**This woman was already making things better. His children were smiling again—and though Noah ached to be a part of it, he wasn't about to blunder in and kill it.**

Jennifer March didn't know he existed, and was showing uncomplicated kindness and fun to his kids. She was showing Tim that some women could show kindness to him without being a threat to his security, and he could almost kiss her for that...

*Don't think of kissing. Don't think of her as a woman at all!*

When she returned from the bathroom, she was still leading Rowdy by the hand...and that look was on her face again. The soft eyes held their own internal struggle.

Jennifer March had ghosts she was refusing to show in front of his kids...yet the hidden pain held Noah with unwilling fascination. Everything she did held his attention, from the smile that lit up her whole face to the gentle sway of her hips as she walked.

**Dear Reader**

When I wrote A MOTHER IN A MILLION, I had no idea it would be one of the first books celebrating Mills & Boon's centenary! I feel very privileged to take part in a celebration of women's fiction, an unashamed love of love that is humankind's most basic need, and epitomises the words 'Mills & Boon'.

From the day my husband encouraged me to write, in 1991, I knew I wanted to be a romance writer. Why? Because from the time I could read romances were what I loved, from *Heidi* and *Little Women* to *Sense and Sensibility* and the other romantic classics. And with Mills & Boon I can write about issues that concern women, while uplifting them with the kind of happy ending we all dream of having for ourselves and our children. I am so proud to take part in this centenary celebration!

I hope you enjoy Noah and Jennifer's story. A happy ending for a man trapped in a life beyond his control, and a woman who no longer believes a happy ending is possible for her, it was the kind of challenge I revel in. If a loved one of yours has gone missing, even for a few days, then I believe you will love this story.

*Melissa*

# A MOTHER
# IN A MILLION

BY
MELISSA JAMES

MILLS & BOON®
*Pure reading pleasure*

First published in Great Britain 2007
Harlequin Mills & Boon Limited,
Eton House, 18-24 Paradise Road, Richmond, Surrey TW9 1SR

© Lisa Chaplin 2007

ISBN: 978 0 263 19727 3

Set in Times Roman 10½ on 12¼ pt
07-1107-53740

Printed and bound in Great Britain
by Antony Rowe Ltd, Chippenham, Wiltshire

**Melissa James** is a mother of three, living in a beach suburb in New South Wales, Australia. A former nurse, waitress, shop assistant, perfume and chocolate demonstrator—among other things—she believes in taking on new jobs for the fun experience. She'll try anything at least once to see what it feels like—a fact that scares her family on regular occasions. She fell into writing by accident, when her husband brought home an article stating how much a famous romance author earned, and she thought, *I can do that!* She can be found most mornings walking and swimming at her local beach with her husband, or every afternoon running around to her kids' sporting hobbies, while dreaming of flying, scuba diving, belaying down a cave or over a cliff—anywhere her characters are at the time!

To two wonderful loving mothers—my own, Mary, and my mother-in-law Rosalie—and to Tania, a mother at last after so many years of suffering. There are many roads to motherhood...

# CHAPTER ONE

"No! NAUGHTY TIMMY. Give back to Rowdy!"

"Make me, loser!"

"I tell Daddy, *bad* boy!"

"Go on, baby," came the taunting older child's voice. "See if Dad cares. See if he even hears you!"

Jennifer March sighed, and laid her latest handmade quilt on her lap. The family next door were at it again. They'd only moved in seven days ago, but she'd heard little except the fighting and yelling. She'd crossed the fence four times to introduce herself, but returned home in silence when she heard the fights or discipline happening at the time.

Given small towns, she could know all about them now, if she chose to; but with all the gossip and speculation she'd endured in her past, she'd preferred to close off confidences, and wait for the people next door to come to her.

So far she'd waited in vain. Maybe they weren't the kind of people to want to introduce themselves to the only neighbour they had—but the kids at least weren't private. The boundary fence lying between her five-acre lot and theirs seemed to be a preferred place to, um, sort out their differences. It wasn't as if she wanted to hear their private business every day.

*Yeah, right. You're going to get involved sooner or later,* an inner voice taunted, not quite bitter nor truly resigned, but something in between. It kind of sounded like Mark, before he'd walked out the final time. *I can't believe you've lasted seven days without waltzing in there to help. Pollyanna strikes again. Go and make everyone's lives better...isn't that why you moved here, to fix Uncle Joe's life after Aunt Jean died?*

She was done fighting with phantoms. Mark could think what he wanted—he would, anyway. If she'd moved here first to help Uncle Joe get through the worst of his grief, she'd also come to escape. Escape the pity...escape her sisters, all having healthy babies around her...

"Daddy *care!*" The baby voice, trembling with emotion, broke into her thoughts. He sounded heartbreakingly like Cody...he must be around three, the same age Cody had been.

They might have played together, though Cody would have been five now.

The familiar lump thickened in her throat, and her eyes stung—but she breathed slowly, in and out, willing control and calm. She'd done her crying. She'd miss Cody until her last breath, would miss being a mother for the rest of her life; but she was making something of herself—

"Yes, Rowdy, Daddy *cares.*" The gravelly voice, grim and tired, pulled Jennifer from the familiar up-down spiral of grief and slow healing.

*Scarring isn't healing, Jen,* Mark would have said. *Get it right.*

"Timothy Brannigan, I'm ashamed of you," the man went on, in a weary mantra. "Teasing a three-year-old. I only asked you to look after your little brother for half an hour while I make up an ad for work. Why did you steal his blanket?"

Before she knew it Jennifer had drifted to the window, watching from behind the curtain. She shouldn't be interested—she should mind her own business…but it wasn't as if entertainment was everywhere up here. Two TV channels, and that was only when the wind was in the right direction or it didn't rain, and the only radio was country music or talkback. *Old man's radio and yee-hah music,* she'd thought when she'd first moved up here from Newcastle for a fresh start. *This really is a two-horse town—two of everything, no more and no less.*

Like these two houses up on the hill overlooking the sea. Twin houses, old and rambling, each on long, thin five-acre blocks five hundred metres from the ocean and three kilometres from town: isolated enough for peace, beautiful enough to fill the spirit.

"I didn't steal it! He was putting it in his mouth, and it's *gross,* Dad." The boy's voice whined as he looked up at his father. "It stinks. Look at the—"

The tall, brown-haired man—he had lovely hair with shimmering golden highlights, even if it was rather shaggy and unkempt—put his hand on the child's shoulder and said in his deep, rumbling voice, "It might be gross to you, Tim, but Rowdy's only little. Now give it back. I'll wash it tomorrow when I do a load." He leaned toward the object of dispute. "It is pretty stinky, isn't it? Rowdy, it gets washed tomorrow."

"Yeah, Timmy," came the baby voice, with cute triumph. "So give back Rowdy's banket!"

"Oh, *have* your stupid baby blanket, then. Get sick, see if I care!"

Tears erupted from the little boy as his brother shoved him along with the blanket to the ground. "Dad-*dee!* Timmy *bad!*"

The pitiful wails were muffled as the man swung the boy up into his arms. Weariness laced his every word as he said, "Tim, time out in your room. Fifteen minutes by the kitchen timer."

"Who cares? There's nothin' to do in this dump anyway! I hate it here. *I hate it!*"

The boy, who looked about seven or eight, stomped off down the hill from the ring of trees where the children had been playing, toward the house next door. The man buried his face in his baby son's soft mess of hair. The little boy's arms wrapped around him; childish hands patted his shoulder blade. The son comforting the father.

From behind the window Jennifer ached, watching the tableau. Poor children—and poor father. He looked exhausted—as stressed as his children appeared to be.

"Where's their mother?" she muttered, aching for them. And wasn't there another child...a girl? She knew she'd seen a tangle-haired moppet wandering around once or twice, golden hair and big blue eyes, like a messy Shirley Temple.

As if in answer, a tiny sniff came from somewhere above Jennifer's head, and then another.

Twisting around under the open sash, she peered through the window. The tangle-haired moppet was up one of Jennifer's trees, a dirty thumb in her mouth and her bright blue eyes like big, serious saucers as she contemplated Jennifer.

*A five-year-old girl was fifteen feet up her tree.*

Panic skittered through her. Jennifer couldn't climb—she'd always been the dollies and tea party kind of little girl, never causing her parents a moment's worry—about her safety, at least. They'd always known where she was, what she was doing—but she was the youngest of four children, the homebody child, and her mother had always been there to watch over them.

*Where was this child's mother?*

Interfering or not, Pollyanna or not, she had to do something... "Hello," she called to the girl, smiling in a way she hoped didn't show her terror. "I'm Jennifer."

The child's mouth tightened around her thumb. She sucked on it with the fury of childhood fear of strangers.

"That's a—a nice tree, isn't it?" Jennifer blathered on as she climbed out the window and walked slowly toward the child. She wouldn't have a clue if it was a nice tree or a killer straight from Hobbiton's Old Forest at the moment, but she had to talk, to connect to the little girl to get her down. "It's my favourite one in the yard."

Nothing.

She craned her neck, looking up at the branch. The little girl was so tiny, and the tree so high… "What's your name?" she asked, beginning to feel desperate—and the little girl's eyes were filling with tears. If her sight blurred and she panicked—

*Please God, I couldn't take another ambulance trip with a dying child!*

"Would you like a cookie?" she cried suddenly, remembering the six-month squirrel's store of cookies in her freezer: her store of rewards and treats for the day-care kids she had four days a week. "Or I could give you some crackers with—with Vegemite? Or chocolate spread?" she asked, thinking of her hidden stash of PMS-rescue spread: the one without nut traces in it, since four-year-old Amy was violently allergic to nuts. For all she knew, this child could be, too.

The little girl's face lit up. "I *like* choc'lit," she confided in a piping voice, as if it were a state secret.

"I have milk, too." Jennifer felt as if she'd scored a major victory.

"*Choc'lit* milk?"

She couldn't help laughing. "I can make chocolate milk, just for you," she agreed, thinking of her other PMS-rescue: her ice-cream syrup. "How does that sound? Is it worth coming down the tree for all that?"

"You said cookie." Her voice was muffled. "A big, fat cookie with choc'lit?"

"You really like chocolate, don't you?" Jennifer said, smiling. "Yes, they're big, fat cookies with *tons* of chocolate chips."

Cody's favourite had been choc-chip cookies, too. Except that Cody wasn't coming back to dunk them in milk and make a mess all over his high chair. Now Ben and Amy and Sascha and Jeremy and Shannon and Cameron sat in that chair—at least in the daytime.

Filling the void with other people's children might be pathetic as Mark had claimed, but at least the void didn't scream at her day and night with its howling emptiness. During the day she had baby hands in hers, big, trusting eyes looking up at her for guidance, fun and games and safety…she was a day-care mother now, and she'd found in the past eighteen months that second-best was far better than nothing at all.

She asked the child, "So is two cookies and chocolate milk worth coming down the tree? Or—or—" she frantically reached for inspiration "—I could make you some spaghetti?"

*Please, just come down before you fall!*

"S'getti?" The little girl sounded ecstatic. "I *like* s'getti."

"Spaghetti and cookies and milk it is, then. What's your name?" she asked again. "I can't make spaghetti and share cookies unless I know your name," she added, laughing. Hoping she would gain the child's trust.

"Cilla," the child said, with a lisp Jennifer didn't know was natural, or caused by the thumb still in her mouth. "Priscilla Amelia Brannigan."

"Well, Priscilla Amelia Brannigan, would you like to come into my kitchen for cookies and chocolate milk and spa-ghetti?" To her intense relief the little girl smiled, pulled her thumb from her mouth and turned to climb down the tree, with a natural agility Jennifer envied.

From the corner of her eye, she saw movement down the hill. The older boy—Tim—was climbing out his bedroom window.

It seemed the man next door had no control over his children whatsoever. It had been less than five minutes, she was sure of that. Surely he must have *seen* the child was feeling so rebellious he wouldn't obey orders for long?

Then a rush of pity filled her, remembering the exhausted, overwhelmed man clinging to a three-year-old for comfort. Before she knew it she was waving the boy over, with a conspiratorial air. Hoping he would come out of curiosity, if nothing else. Someone had to help that poor man—*I mean, the poor children.*

"Catch me!"

On instinct, her arms reached out—and a moment later, her arms were full of warm, silky-soft skin, and the scent of muddy child and baby shampoo filled her head.

She minded other people's children every day, held them when they hurt or to carry them around—so what was it about this child's touch that choked her up so tight she couldn't *breathe?*

She put Cilla down to the ground with care, before she dropped her; the trembling, when it came, was bone-deep.

"Cookie?" The hopeful voice woke her from the half-dreaming world of loss. Big, trusting eyes were shining as she looked up at Jennifer.

She pulled herself together, as she'd done every day of the past eighteen months, when she'd decided she could either sink into terminal depression, or try to make something good from the ashes of her life. "Cookie," she said, smiling. "Let's go wash your face and hands first."

A little warm hand slipped into hers. "Timmy wants a cookie, too." Cilla pointed to the boundary fence, where a very dirty face was peeking through the wooden rail slats.

Again, though she held other children's hands almost every day, the feel of Cilla's hand in hers filled her heart with her sweet trust, poignant with memory—with the need for motherhood she must deny for the rest of her life.

*Stop it.* She turned her face, and smiled at the wary, hostile little boy peering at her as if he expected her to yell at him. "So you're Tim," she said gravely.

The boy nodded, his chin pushed out. Pugnacious and ready to fight. "I'm eight," he said aggressively, as if she was about to argue the fact.

"I'm Jennifer, your neighbour. I bet you like spaghetti and choc-chip cookies, too." She grinned down at Cilla as her brother scrambled over the fence in record time—and, watching the child, Jennifer realised how thin he was. Lean, hungry, wary with suffering and only eight...

She'd had every intention of sending Tim back to his room to wait out the fifteen minutes of wholesome discipline, telling him the food would be waiting when he'd obeyed his father. As a child-care worker, she knew reinforcing parental commands was vital. Yet Jennifer found herself saying, "Then come on in."

*Yeah, right, Jen. You were never going to send him back.*

Her mouth curved into a determined smile as she led the way in.

Somehow she didn't think Tim would take well to being told to wash his face and hands; so she led Cilla into the bathroom, and hoped he'd get the message.

He didn't. They returned to the kitchen to find him sitting at the table. The look on his face was daring her to even *think* about ordering him to the bathroom.

But she'd had a better idea, based on the reactions of Shannon, the livewire child she minded every Tuesday and Thursday. With a lifted brow, she tossed a warm wet cloth on the table *splat* in front of him, and stood there, waiting. *Do it.*

Tim didn't move to touch the cloth. He folded his arms and waited, his expression matching hers. *Make me.*

A tiny tug at her hand made Jennifer look down at Cilla. Her little face—so pretty, now she could see it without smudges everywhere—was hopeful. "I'm *very* hungry… and I washed."

Jennifer smiled. "You're right, Cilla." She opened the fridge and freezer, got out plates, and put two cookies in the microwave to soften while she made up the chocolate milk.

One glass. One plate.

She settled Cilla with her snack. "There you are, sweetie." She turned back to put away the food on the bench. "I wouldn't even think about it if I were you, Tim," she remarked placidly.

A stifled gasp told her she'd been right; he'd been about to steal Cilla's food and run.

"The milk and cookies will be out on this bench for another thirty seconds—and remember, you can come back every day for more…if you wash first," she announced to no one in particular, and checked her watch. "Twenty-two…twenty-five…"

*Thwap!* She gasped as the washcloth landed on the curve of her neck and shoulder.

She ought to have *known* a fighter like Tim wouldn't be able to resist! She fought to keep calm, but a laugh burst out of her. Turning, she saw a clean face filled with mischievous challenge and wary defensiveness, unsure if he was about to be disciplined by a stranger.

She plucked the cloth from her shoulder and threw it back, landing right on his head.

Cilla laughed and clapped, spitting cookie bits all over the table. "Get her back, Timmy!"

Tim grinned and threw the cloth. He laughed when Jennifer staggered back, coughing and wiping her mouth as if the dirt from his face had gone in.

Cilla choked on enchanting laughter when Jennifer threw the cloth at her. She tossed it on to Tim, who threw it at Jennifer.

The room erupted in laughter and dirty wet-washer attacks.

From outside the back door, a sleepy Rowdy on his hip, Noah Brannigan watched the scene. He'd seen Tim heading for the fence, and came to fetch him back—but now all he could do was stare through the screen, with a joy so poignant it was almost pain. Tim was *laughing*.

It had been exactly three years since he'd seen his boy so— *little*. A child having fun, just because he could. No reason...

And Cilla was here, too—*Cilla*, so shy she never spoke to him, her own dad, without her thumb in her mouth, and who never talked to strangers. Cilla had been disappearing every day since they moved from Sydney to Hinchliff, and Noah hadn't been able to find her. He only wished he understood why Cilla had become so silent, so reclusive.

She wasn't merely speaking now; she was *shrieking* with joy, her big eyes alight as she spat cookie crumbs across the table. She took her turn tossing the grubby washcloth at the woman, who cried foul with a grin and tossed it at Tim, who dodged it and caught it with one hand, throwing it back at their neighbour. The woman, after a pitiful attempt at dodging in turn, took it on the chin. Literally. Her face was alight with mirth.

Who'd have thought his kids would finally find laughter in a game of tag-teaming with a dirty face cloth?

"They're having fun, Daddy," Rowdy whispered from Noah's shoulder.

"Yes, they are," he whispered back, the gratitude a deep ache inside him.

"Want cookie, too. Want—" Rowdy wriggled down from his hip and raced inside, sure of his welcome. "Rowdy want cookie," he announced.

Jennifer March—he'd heard about her from Henry, the local mechanic and jack-of-all-fixing, and one of the best gossips in town—had peeled the wet cloth from her face, and turned to Noah's son with a flitting expression he couldn't identify. It lasted only a moment, before she smiled and took his hand. "Then we'd better get you washed, Rowdy, and you and Tim can both have your cookies."

Almost casually, she tossed the washcloth a final time at Tim, and poked her tongue out in cheeky victory as she led Rowdy into the bathroom.

Noah knew enough about the woman next door, from the people in town. She was divorced, in her late twenties, and the only provider of child-care in town. Yet, from the moment he'd seen her in the distance, he'd refused to go over to introduce himself and the kids, as good manners demanded. Even from that distance, there was *something*...

A quiet, restful woman who could often be seen wearing simple cotton sundresses and sandals, her hair almost always in a loose plait. She seemed to have a natural connection to the children she minded; they followed her around like the Pied Piper—and his kids felt it, too, even from a distance. The laughter and games emanating from the house up the hill drew the kids to play at the ring of trees near the boundary fence every day.

But for him, she wasn't restful. There was something about her...

He had little choice now but to go inside—and unless he could hide the way he looked at Jennifer March, disaster would follow the introduction. For the past three years, Tim's terrified preoccupation that his dad would remarry had reached epic proportions. He'd appointed himself his father's personal watchdog, using his worst behaviour to scare off any woman who came within thirty feet of Noah, unless she was old or married. If a woman got up the courage to flirt with him, his son's pitiful, terror-filled nightmares were more than Noah could stand. *Make her go away, Dad, or Mummy will never come home…*

Little did Tim know; there was no question of his remarriage for a long time. While Belinda was missing she couldn't sign divorce papers, and until seven years had passed, he was as bound to his marriage as if Belinda was still sharing his life and bed. He could force a divorce—but at what cost? Peter and Jan wouldn't allow him to divorce their daughter without causing a fuss the size of Uluru, and Noah refused to allow anything to damage the kids further.

So he was stuck in this limbo, needing help but unable to reach out to any woman who could mother the kids for another four years. Even if Noah *wanted* a woman in his life, Tim would never accept a woman that wasn't his mother. Poor little man, he'd suffered so much the past three years. The child psychologist said the acting out was a combination of grief and terror of losing him, his only security. He'd counselled patience—that this would be a long-term problem until Tim could stand at Belinda's grave and begin to find healing through closure.

The counsellor was right. Tim still checked inside every passing car, looked in every store or on the street, for signs of Belinda. Noah had lost that luxury over a year ago. He was too busy trying to keep his family together and pay off debts; but somehow he'd find a way to make things better.

This woman was already making things better. Tim and Cilla were smiling again—and though he ached to be a part of it, he wasn't about to blunder in and kill it.

Jennifer March didn't know he existed, and was showing uncomplicated kindness and fun to his kids. She was showing Tim that some women could show kindness to him without being a threat to his security, and he could almost kiss her for that…

*Don't think of kissing. Don't think of her as a woman at all!*

When she returned from the bathroom, she was still leading Rowdy by the hand…and that look was on her face again. The soft eyes held their own internal struggle.

Jennifer March had ghosts she was refusing to show in front of his kids…yet the hidden pain held Noah with unwilling fascination. Everything she did held his attention, from the smile that lit up her whole face to the gentle sway of her hips as she walked.

She put Rowdy in the high chair beside the table, and strapped him safely in. "Right, boys, it's time for your cookies."

Cilla sniffled. Noah's gaze swivelled to his daughter. She'd lowered her eyes to the table top, her thumb shoved in her mouth; and he ached for his daughter's inability to ask, like a normal child. Following her big brother's example of silence, and expecting nothing. He hated that Cilla and Tim weren't normal kids—but he didn't have the weapons for that particular fight. It was all he could do to keep the family together.

Until those final few months after Rowdy's birth, when the post-natal depression took her over, Belinda had been a fantastic mother. She'd have known how to fix Tim and Cilla. She wouldn't have made one fumbling mistake after another.

Jennifer March had already turned to Cilla, with a smile and wink—and Noah caught his breath with the gentle sweetness of those thick-lashed blue eyes and curving pink lips. "I think someone's still hungry." The words held conspiratorial fun, not rebuke; and Cilla responded to it. The thumb stayed in, but she nodded, smiling around the hand half-shoved inside.

Jennifer turned back to the bench, her hair swinging around her shoulder as she did. Shiny brown hair half-spilled from a loose plait reaching her shoulder blades. She had a dusting of freckles across a slightly long nose, and across lightly tanned oval cheeks. Her figure, encased in plain jeans and a purple T-shirt, was ordinary—curvy without being slender or voluptuous.

There was nothing spectacular about Jennifer March: just an average woman. Yet as she looked down at Cilla, her smile—so tender and caring—made her something deeper, richer than beautiful. The sight of her with his kids did something, not just to his body, but to his heart. Like a funny tug, warm and soft. Safe, and yet—

He shook his head to clear it. He didn't like the stray thoughts he'd been getting about her. He hadn't been with a woman since Belinda's disappearance three years ago, and he didn't *want* his body to wake up from its somnolence. It was a complication he didn't need.

It seemed he had no choice. He'd moved to Hinchliff for change—and he'd got it. He was living next door to a woman he already found compelling. The worst part was, she hadn't even said a word to him yet. What would happen once they met? And if Tim picked up on it...

*Get over yourself, Brannigan. She might not even like you.*

He wasn't stupid enough to think he was a prize to any woman. He was still putting a new architectural and building business in place after having to sell off his Sydney operation to pay the debts, most of which he'd only discovered after Belinda was gone; he had three kids he was barely coping with. If only he'd *seen* the depth of Belinda's depression.

"Hmmm." Jennifer checked her watch as she put more cookies in the microwave, and stirred chocolate sauce into the milk. "You know what, Priscilla Amelia? It's almost lunchtime. I think it's time I made that alphabet spaghetti for everyone."

"Yeah!" Rowdy cried, who knew what the alphabet was from *Sesame Street,* and loved spaghetti in any form. "Alpaget p's'getti!"

"Then more cookies?" Cilla mumbled around her thumb.

"Then more cookies," Jennifer replied. Her mouth twitched, but she kept a straight face. "We'd better let your mum and dad know where you are, though. Tim, could you—"

"My mummy's dead," Cilla said without expression—just stating a fact.

Noah, knowing what was about to happen, closed his eyes, and sent up a desperate, heartfelt prayer for help, knowing it wouldn't help. Nothing could.

About to say something—probably an apology, but what a *terrible* introduction to his family!—Jennifer was interrupted by Tim's snapping, "Mummy's *not* dead! She was sad, and she went away for a while. She'll come back!"

Cilla just looked at Tim, her big eyes holding a world of unspoken sorrow. She didn't say anything—she knew Tim would.

"Shut up, thumb-sucker. She will find us, she will!" Tim yelled. "Even if we're like *days* away from home now! Nana and Pa know where we are. She said she'd come back."

"I don't got a mummy," Rowdy said, his big, trusting eyes on Jennifer, who was hurrying to bring the cookies over.

"Yeah, that's 'cause you made her run off, loser," Tim muttered. He crammed a cookie in his mouth, gulped down the milk and turned to get out of the house.

His mother's son: when things get too hard, bolt...

Noah rapped on the old, ratty screen door before Tim could make his getaway. "Hello," he called. "I see my kids have found free food with all their usual skill." He made the tone joking—or tried to, but it fell as flat as the atmosphere inside the big, homey old country kitchen.

Tim's look was pure accusation. He knew he was about to be disciplined, and attack was his best form of defence.

Half of Cilla's hand disappeared into her mouth; the pitiful shaking came back. Within moments she, too, would disappear—and Noah had no way to cure her. It scared the living daylights out of him every time she went missing, and if he tried to make her understand he wasn't angry, just terrified, it led to tears and heartbreaking apologies. *I'm sorry I'm a bad girl, Daddy. Please don't go away like Mummy!*

"Come on in, Mr. Brannigan, and have a cookie. I'm just about to warm a new batch for the kids," Jennifer said with utter calm—and the evil spell disintegrated as if it had never been. Her gaze on him was more compelling than words. *Help me out here.* "Would you like a cup of tea or coffee with that? Or maybe you want chocolate milk, too?"

Caught out by the teasing, Tim sniggered at his father. "Dad makes the *worst* chocolate milk," he mock-complained. "He makes it so milky you can't find the chocolate."

"Then maybe I'd better get another bottle of chocolate sauce out, and show him how it's done?" she suggested, smiling as if the eruption over Belinda's disappearance had never taken place. "Or does he spill the milk, too? Mr. Dropsy Brannigan?"

Cilla giggled...*Cilla giggled.*

Noah wanted to take Jennifer March in his arms—no, to go into her arms, lay his head on her shoulder and thank her from his soul for the gift she'd just given Cilla. His serious, hurting baby was laughing, and he wanted to shout with joy.

"Actually, it's *Noah* Dropsy Brannigan," he said, gruff with the emotion filling his throat.

"I'm very pleased to meet you, Mr. Noah Dropsy Brannigan." As the kids giggled again, Jennifer smiled and pulled out a chair for him. "I'm Jennifer March."

The gentle, light-up-the-room smile had finally turned his way, and it socked him in the guts with its power. Was it her, or this place? Like a wave of a fairy godmother's wand, like they'd been transported to a magical place where no pain existed, his family had become *normal* from the moment they'd stepped inside Jennifer March's door.

Looking at her, he also felt normal…just an ordinary guy for once…and it was good.

He smiled, wondering if she'd known his name all along, as he had hers. The bush telegraph of local gossip ran pretty fast in country towns. "Pleased to meet you, too, Ms Jennifer *I make great chocolate milk* March."

The kids laughed again—they'd laughed *with* him as well as *at* him…

His kids were laughing, just like any other kids.

As he sat at the plain wooden chair, a scent surrounded him: chocolate, vanilla and cookies, furniture polish and fresh air. The walls were scattered with Wiggles posters, times tables and fun alphabet pictures as well as simply framed long-stitch pictures of old houses. The floor in the next room had a big, fluffy old rainbow rug that just begged kids to play on it.

Despite the seeming absence of a child—maybe it was with its father right now?—Jennifer March must be a mother. No day-care place he'd used in Sydney felt like this house. It had the aura and scent of old-fashioned love and motherhood and comfort—of *home*.

It was an aura the kids were responding to with instinctive enthusiasm. All three of them kept their eyes on Jennifer as if she'd disappear if they didn't—especially Cilla and Rowdy, neither of whom could remember Belinda.

Tim was another, infinitely sadder matter. Although it was obvious he liked Jennifer's cookies and her gentle way of dealing with his rebellion, the wariness in his eyes, as they flicked between Jennifer March and his dad, told its tale. The adored mother he'd done his best to protect from her depression had left them with a fourteen-year-old girl, walked out of the house and never returned…

But she would always be his mum. Tim was still on guard, protecting the family as Belinda had asked him to. It was a sacred vow to him. *Watch the kids until I get back, honey.*

Instead of playing at soldiers with toys, Tim was a soldier in a war without detente. That his little son should know such weary fear and endless vigilance at eight years old made Noah want to weep tears of blood. So many useless nights of little sleep, trying to work out a way to heal him. Trying to work out *why* Belinda had ever left.

But these days, he understood the need to run away from your life, no matter how much you love your family. But that she'd never returned, never once checked on the kids she adored—

Only one answer made sense, but how could he *know?* If in three long years—one thousand and forty-five days—he'd had a letter, just one call, he might *believe...*

On the three-year anniversary of Belinda's disappearance he couldn't stand it anymore. He'd sold the house in western Dural and headed seven hundred kilometres north of Sydney to Hinchliff. Selling everything off paid the debts he still hadn't cleared. He'd bought the house next door for little more than a song, hoping the change of scene and people—and distance from Belinda's obsessive, eternally grieving parents—would help bring his family some closure.

But now, seven hundred kilometres from Sydney and all its sad memories, he knew it would take nothing less than a miracle to bring the Brannigan nightmare to an end.

But then, hadn't he just witnessed a miracle, right here in Jennifer March's kitchen? His kids were *playing* for the first time in three years...and he was terrified to take them home, and face the reality that was just too damn painful.

# CHAPTER TWO

NOAH *DROPSY* BRANNIGAN had the worst kind of smile.

The kind that made her forget what she was doing, right in the middle of doing it.

That was bad. Really bad—because she hadn't had that kind of reaction to a man since Mark McBride had walked into her life when she was seventeen. And he'd walked right back out seven years later, three months before Cody had his final attack, and all the medication in the world hadn't been enough to make him breathe again.

Her right fist clenched hard to stop the shaking. She looked down at it in the usual half-disbelieving revulsion. It had been happening for two years, just like that. Why was it only *one* of her hands trembled? It was as if she were having a one-sided brain malfunction. She'd done all she could to return to a normal life. She'd accepted the past—and her future. She was a genetic Cystic Fibrosis carrier, and until they found a cure, she couldn't risk having more kids. Mark, a recessive carrier, was long gone, living a far less complicated life.

Her world was slow, placid and serene. She didn't want anything more to complete it. She was happy enough.

So why did her right hand continue to betray her this way?

"Where the alpaget p's'getti?"

The sound of the baby voice worked on the shaking as if it were medicine. Jennifer found she could look up again; she even smiled. "I'm sorry, Rowdy. I promised, didn't I? Alphabet spaghetti, coming right up." Trying to prove her control had returned, she pulled her pot drawer open with more force than necessary; and because it was an old dove-tailed drawer without protective wheels and pulleys it flew out hard, too fast to stop.

She landed in a heap on the floor with the big old drawer on top of her, the sound of pots clanking against the tiled floor hurting her ears, the wind knocked out of her and pain shooting up from her tailbone to her back and palms.

All three kids burst into giggles. "Look at her! She got pots all over her!" Rowdy chortled.

The drawer was lifted from her within seconds, and her hands taken in a warm, strong clasp. "Are you okay, Jennifer? Do you hurt anywhere? Can you stand up?"

"I—don't know. I think—" No…she wasn't thinking, because she *couldn't* think. His hands enveloping hers made her feel strange…mushy and warm and safe. And—and—

Strong hands. Builder's hands, sturdy and capable, like his body…lithe and muscular and—and dependable.

*Yes, you fooled yourself just the same way with Mark, didn't you?*

"Jennifer? Should I get a doctor?"

Dazed, she stared up at Noah. His strong brown face was filled with concern, his eyes—oh, they were deep, warm brown, almost like maple syrup: a shade darker than his sun-kissed hair. So gentle, yet so—*powerful.* Like his smile…

"No, I'm okay," she said, but heard the breathlessness: an instinctive female-touching-attractive-male reaction she hadn't felt in years.

She was on her feet again. How did that happen? One

moment she was on the floor, her hands in Noah's, and now she was standing.

"Are you sure you're okay? You don't seem very steady." He put a hand at her back as he turned her to a seat. "Maybe you should sit down?"

It was only then she realised one of her hands still clung to his; she couldn't stop looking at him. A dim part of her acknowledged what he was saying—yes, *unsteady* was a good term for her shaky grip on uprightness. But she didn't know if that was due to the fall, or the effect this man was having on her.

"Apart from my lacerated dignity, I'm fine," she said ruefully, smiling at him, "and, um, sitting down might hurt more than it would help right now."

"Gotcha." He grinned, and her breath caught again.

"Thank you…Noah," she said softly, wondering why she'd ever preferred chocolate syrup on pancakes to maple; it was the most beautiful colour, um, taste, um—

"Dad, stop it *now!*"

The words were a reprimand, a command. Jennifer watched as Noah's eyes clouded over with a pain that seemed older than he was himself, sadder than the world should have to carry.

*His wife. His children's mother.* Oh God, help her, what had she been *thinking? He's a married man, no matter where his wife is. If he hasn't divorced her, he isn't free.*

He released his hold on her and turned to Tim, gentle and sad, yet with a dignity she found compelling to watch. "Tim, you're being rude and ungrateful. We're in Jennifer's house, eating her food, and she hurt herself. She needed help."

From stark-white, the boy flushed, and looked down at the table. "You didn't have to—" He didn't say it, but the words almost shimmered in front of them all: a neon sign of resentment. *You didn't have to touch her.*

With those words, Jennifer had gone from friend to enemy in the eyes of a small child who wanted his mummy home again.

"Yes, I did." Noah was gentle, and unutterably weary; as if it was an argument they'd danced their way through many times before. "And if you don't know why, I've failed to teach you any good manners. Jennifer's been kind to you all. Did you expect me to leave her on the floor, hurt?"

Tim didn't look up, didn't speak; but Noah's quiet dignity and strength as he dealt with his rebellious son mesmerised her. The *love* for his ungracious, hurting child all but shimmered from him, giving him an aura as warm and caramelly as his eyes.

Still, she ached for this family Ring Around the Rosie, which could go nowhere but to the eventual falling down. Yet she knew better than to interfere. What she didn't know would definitely hurt her in this case—or it would hurt others. It wasn't her place to blunder in.

Strange, but it felt as if Noah's lost wife was standing in the room with them. Her presence in Tim's heart was so real, so vivid Jennifer could almost see her.

"Tim, apologise to Jennifer," Noah was saying, his voice both gentle and inflexible.

"No! I don't want her stupid spaghetti anyway. This place *sucks!*" Shoving his chair back with ferocious force, Tim bolted from the house.

The chair tottered and fell to the floor with a crash that almost seemed an anti-climax.

Cilla sucked on her thumb as if her life depended on it. Rowdy just stared at his father with a sympathy more deep and heartfelt than any three-year-old should know. "We get Timmy, Daddy?" he asked quietly, as if it was something they'd done many times before.

Not knowing what else to do, Jennifer picked up a pot from the floor and crossed to the sink to fill it with water for the pasta.

"Jennifer—ah, Ms March—"

Hearing the anguished awkwardness of an apology unspoken—of the distance he was forced to put between them— she turned to smile at him. "I have spaghetti sauce all ready, Mr. Brannigan. I just need to heat it. Why don't you leave Cilla and Rowdy here with me, and spend some time with Tim?"

Noah's face darkened. He said nothing, but she could feel the indecision, fear and hope.

"I'm a qualified child-carer, Mr. Brannigan, as well as your neighbour. As you might have noticed, I run a day-care centre from home. I'm licensed to have up to six children here at a time," she said, in her most professional tone. "Feel free to call Fred Sherbrooke, the local police sergeant, to verify my capability. The number's on the wall beside the phone."

His jaw hardened. "I can't afford to pay you."

So that was the reason for his hesitation. How hard it must have been for him to say that. She clenched her fists against the useless wish to cover his hand with hers. Cilla or Rowdy could tell Tim of it later, and it was obvious the boy was threat- ened—or scared—enough. "We're neighbours, Mr. Brannigan, and I invited you all for lunch. I'm not going anywhere else today. I've been to my Sunday service." *Please go. Your son needs you! Can't you see he needs you to run after him?*

She'd said all she could without crossing the line. The rest was up to him.

With a short nod, he got to his feet. "Thank you."

"Spaghetti will be waiting for you both, if Tim wants to come back," she called after him as he ran down the back stairs.

The screen door swung shut: the only answer she received.

After a short silence where Jennifer scrambled to say some- thing, the only noise was of Cilla sucking her thumb with greater force.

"Are we ready for spaghetti?" she finally asked with a

brightness they all knew was overdone. Cilla wrapped her thumb-sucking hand around her nose, covering half her face—and little Rowdy looked up at Jennifer with big, candid eyes.

"Timmy gets mad a lot," he said quietly.

Two hours later, having called Tim's phone every ten minutes—it was switched off again—having been to every place Tim had run to since they'd moved here, combing every tree, every inch of the beach, even driving a few miles in each direction of the Pacific Highway, Noah called Sergeant Sherbrooke to tell him Tim had disappeared again.

Fred didn't make the joke about needing a leash for his kids this time, or ask which trees he'd checked out so far. The jokes had stopped when Fred had checked the COPS database, and found out about Belinda—and Noah didn't know which he hated more, the jokes or the awkward silences filled with pity.

He'd given the details to Fred and Mandy, the uniformed woman with him. She'd said in a town the size of Hinchliff it would only take an hour or two. Since it was Sunday, more recruits were available to make the calls, and to get out and search in all the likely kid places.

Noah trudged toward the house next door to get Cilla and Rowdy before heading back out to look everywhere a second time, and try again.

From experience, he knew Tim would only return in his own time and way—Noah hoped to God he would, anyway. He couldn't fool himself he was overreacting, when he wasn't. This constant fear was so much harder to take for its not being groundless. Every time Tim ran away or Cilla vanished, another chunk of him seemed to crumble into dust. His life revolved around keeping his family together, but it just kept disintegrating before his eyes.

As he drew nearer to the March house, a squeal of laughter

lifted his soul for a moment—just a moment. Why the hell had he shown up here earlier today? Jennifer had proven herself capable of dealing with his kids—far more than he was—and Tim would still be here, safe and happy, if he hadn't stuck his nose in.

If he could, he'd turn and leave at this moment, leave Cilla and Rowdy here, laughing and joyous, and help the townfolk to find Tim; but it wasn't up to him. Jennifer—Ms March—had a life of her own to live, and it didn't include unlimited, unpaid babysitting.

No matter how *happy* she made his kids.

A shriek filled the air, followed by the slamming of the screen door. Jennifer came flying out, her long plait streaked with garish rainbow shades of paint, screaming with laughter. Cilla and Rowdy followed within moments, brandishing paintbrushes aloft in teasing threat.

Jennifer—he couldn't think of her as Ms March, looking like that—caught sight of him. She grinned and waved as she bolted past him and into the ring of trees halfway to the boundary fence, squealing like the proverbial stuck pig, arms waving madly. "You can't get me again!" she cried, dodging between trees at little-kid pace.

Cilla and Rowdy bolted straight past him, yelling, "We're gonna get you!"

After playing dodge-paintbrush for a few minutes she allowed them to "get" her, falling to the ground and allowing them to daub her with yet more riotous colours. Cilla and Rowdy were yelling like victorious warriors as they dug the paintbrushes into her hair and face.

"Wait, wait!" she cried after a minute or two, with a massive grin. "You win!"

The kids gave blood-curdling bellows, sitting on her belly, holding their paintbrushes aloft as if they were Excalibur.

"We're the champions!" they chortled while she mock-bucked, trying to get up.

When it came to children, Jennifer March obviously gave no thought to her dignity—and his kids responded to her brand of fun like winter buds finding sunlight and rain.

Earlier, when assuring Noah he could trust Jennifer with his kids, Fred had told him she lived alone. Why *wasn't* she a mother? So what if she was divorced? She was pretty and gentle and fun-loving, so why hadn't some other man snapped her up long before now?

Then, remembering the flashes of sadness in her eyes, he knew there must be a compelling reason why she was spending her life minding other people's kids instead of having her own.

He shook himself. It wasn't his place to find out Jennifer March's past. He had enough trouble trying to work out how to make his kids happy; and from bitter experience he knew he was no good at working out what a woman was thinking, let alone how to make her life work.

He'd get past this brief fascination with Jennifer March, become friends with her, and the man in him would go back to sleep. He had no choice but to believe that.

Sudden tugging at his jeans made him look down. "Daddy, did you see? Daddy, we won!"

Seeing his little son's eager excitement, Noah grinned and swung Rowdy up on his hip. "I saw, matey. You and Cilla are the paint warriors! Yah!" He gave his best attempt at a blood-curdling scream of victory.

"Aaah, Daddy, ouch!" Rowdy covered his ears, grinning.

But Cilla's thumb shoved back in her mouth as she looked at her father; her eyes were big with a fear he *couldn't* have inspired in her. He'd never even been able to bring himself to tap her hand, his fragile little girl. *Why* was she frightened of him? What was it that made him such a damn *failure* with his kids?

The feminine voice called out cheerfully, "Right, who wants to turn my boring pink Play-Doh into a rainbow?"

"Me! Me! C'mon, Cilla, let's go!" Rowdy wriggled until Noah let him down—and Cilla was smiling again, her eyes filled with an excitement he couldn't manage to rouse in her with all his play ideas.

"Sit at the table. I'll come in a minute and get it down for you. Just grab more paper and keep painting until I get there," Jennifer called after them as both ran for the house.

When they'd gone, she came to him—too close—and laid a hand on his arm, her multihued face filled with concern. "You couldn't find Tim?"

Something flashed through him at the touch, just as it had earlier when he'd lifted her to her feet. He didn't know what it was, besides the obvious male reaction to a pretty woman in his vicinity—and he didn't want to know. It was useless anyway. He'd met the woman for the first time three hours ago and she was already babysitting for him and—

*Feeling sorry for him.*

*Yeah, let's help the emotional basket case before he screws his kids up any worse than he already has.*

He pulled his arm out from under her hand, hoping the move was subtle, so she wouldn't think he was running scared. "He'll come home when he's ready. He always does." His mouth tightened. *That's it, tell the woman your son disappears all the time, why don't you?*

"If he does this—" she hesitated "—does he have a phone?"

"Yes," he sighed, and ran a hand through his hair. "It's off."

"I see," she said quietly, and he had the feeling she really did see—too much. "Did you call Fred Sherbrooke?"

"Of course I did. Tim's only eight," he snapped.

"Of course you did. Stupid question," she murmured; but something in her voice made him look closer at her. Well, he'd wanted the concern and pity gone from her face, hadn't he? Mission accomplished. Beneath the mess of paint streaks, the pretty, gentle face was emotionless, but the lack of expression was a touch overdone. "I'd better take the plastic off the Play-Doh for the kids, and put it on the Formica table. I'll be right back."

The distance lay between them like the universe, or a time paradox. She was here, yet she wasn't. He got the point; he even appreciated it. She could keep as much distance from him as she liked, so long as she was good to his kids.

"No need. I'll take the kids off your hands." He almost winced at the flat hardness of his tone. "You've done more than enough already."

"And I'm a stranger," she said, still neutral. "But I promised them. You're welcome to take some of the Play-Doh and paint home for the kids, if you prefer. I have plenty here." She turned and strode for the house, not a single feminine sway about it.

That much he understood. He'd made her angry, but she wasn't going to talk about it, because despite all she'd done for him, they were strangers.

She was a stranger who'd been nothing but kind to him, and he'd not only rebuffed her kindness, he'd thrown it back in her face. He'd doused her in cold water: a punishment that belonged to other times and other people. She hadn't interfered.

He watched her go, conscious of a wish to call her back and apologise.

*You owe her that much, at the very least. And you're good at apologies—remember? You had good experience every time you got it wrong with Belinda.*

Wishing he had a clue what made women tick, he sighed and walked in after her.

Inside the kitchen, the withdrawn woman she'd been with him moments before had vanished. She was warm and laughing again as she packed a lump of Play-Doh and a small package of paints for the kids.

Was she in such total control of her emotions as this? Could she be? Heaven knew if she was he'd bottle whatever it was she had, and drink it every day. If he could show his kids nothing but warmth and laughter, Tim and Cilla might actually want to hang around with him.

"Here you are, Play-Doh and paint and brushes. If you lay it on a sheet of plastic, and watch them—"

"I have a play mat," he said, breaking into her words with a curtness she didn't deserve, and again, her face closed off. "I'm sorry," he sighed, turning away. "I'm worried."

"You wouldn't be human if you weren't." Her voice was strange as she added, too soft for the kids to hear, "I know you don't think so at the moment, but you *are* a good father. It's obvious how much you love your kids. Tim will come home."

"You don't know anything about what I'm thinking or feeling," he snapped, wanting to hit himself within moments. "Look—"

"It's okay, Mr. Brannigan," she said quietly. "I don't appreciate others prying into my personal business, either. I obviously crossed the line. I'm sorry, too."

He nodded, relief filling him at the understanding that didn't descend to pity; but then, looking into her eyes—soft and pretty and glimmering with a world of pain unspoken—he said gruffly, "Too many people knew my business back home."

After a long silence, she said in almost a whisper, "You're not the only one."

She'd turned away before he could ask and on second thought, he didn't want to know. It wasn't as if *he* could help; he couldn't even keep his kids at home. "We'd better go."

She nodded, her head drooping a little. "I'll keep an eye out here. I'll call Fred if Tim comes home, okay?"

He wanted to thank her for the help, but all he could see was Jennifer standing alone, watching through windows for his son because she had nothing else to fill her Sunday nights...or any nights.

For the first time in a long time, he wondered if the peace of being alone could replace the feeling of little arms around his neck; if the quiet of no kid fights was worth rising and eating, cooking and cleaning for one only. She seemed so alone...yet she hadn't said a word.

"Goodbye," she said softly.

On impulse, he took her hand in his. "Thank you for everything, Jennifer."

She didn't answer, but the stiffness of her back at his touch spoke a thousand words—and this time, he wished he couldn't read a woman.

She wanted him to take his kids and leave.

Leave her alone in this empty house: a home made for fun and family and laughter and love, holding one solitary woman with sadness in soft blue eyes and no one to give all that joy and laughter to...

Suddenly, for no reason he could fathom, he said, "I like a quiet glass of wine in the back paddock at night when the kids are asleep. If you'd like to join me tonight, I'd—"

She whirled back around to face him, eyes burning with fury that didn't even seem funny with the paint still daubing her face and hair. She snapped before he could finish the sentence, "You're right, Mr. Brannigan, I don't know much about you—but I do know you have a wife, wherever she is."

The fury swamping him, the overwhelming anger at the judgment when he was scared out of his mind for Tim, was too white-hot to think about how he'd put the invitation. "I might not win the world's greatest father award, or the world's strongest moralist, but you can at least acquit me of adultery.

I chose not to bring up my private business in casual conversation with a stranger while my kids were listening—" he quickly turned his head to check where Cilla and Rowdy were completely absorbed in painting, before he went on in a low voice "—especially with Tim still needing to believe his mum will come home. But in three years, Belinda hasn't used a credit card, hasn't touched her bank accounts, hasn't been seen anywhere. Even if she'd left *me,* she was a devoted mother and daughter, and she hasn't contacted her kids or her parents. The police marked her file 'presumed dead' over a year ago."

She caught her breath—a little, strangled gasp. "I'm *sorry,*" she whispered, her soft-tanned face pale with shock.

He barely heard the apology; his chest heaving as if he'd run a race, he said, low, "Just so you know, the offer was my way of thanking you for minding the kids and for your hospitality. There's nothing I can do to repay you for today, but I wanted to give back—maybe friendship. I have nothing else to give a woman. Whatever you might think of me, I wouldn't sink so low as to hit on a neighbour I've just met, especially when you've been kind to me and my kids."

No longer pale, a deep, burning blush filled her face. Her eyes glimmered with tears. "I don't want repayment…Noah," she whispered. With an averted face, she held out her hand. "Can we go back a few minutes? I'd love a glass of wine…"

Just like that, his fury evaporated. Remembering everything she'd done for him today, all the kindness he'd just thrown in her face as a punishment for a misunderstanding not of her making. With a rueful smile, he took her hand. "Friends?"

"Yes, please." She still couldn't look at him—and her hand was shaking.

What to say? He didn't know her well enough to know in what way he'd upset her most—he only knew he felt like a first-class loser right now. "Jennifer…"

"What time will I come over?" she said softly. "I wouldn't want to come too early, and upset Tim."

*Tim.* He'd wasted fifteen minutes here that he could have spent searching for his son...

"Try about nine. I have to go now. Kids, we have to find Timmy, and get some dinner." He snapped his fingers, and Cilla and Rowdy got to their feet. They never argued or disobeyed his orders when Tim disappeared again; they knew he must be found.

At that moment, the phone rang. As Jennifer moved to answer it, he packed up the presents she'd given him for the kids, and tilted his head toward the door.

"Noah, wait!"

He turned back, seeing a radiant smile covering her face. "Tim's been found."

# CHAPTER THREE

IT WAS almost half-past nine when he finally walked out his back door.

Watching from where she sat on a rocking swing on her side verandah, Jennifer waited another minute before rising to her feet. She didn't want to seem anxious—as if she saw him and ran for him. As if she saw him as something more than just a new neighbour.

As if he were a man she felt compelled to reach out to, to be with, even when the reminders of his runaway wife cast a shadow so dark she could barely see the man he'd been.

A runaway wife, a runaway son…but she refused to judge him as the cause of both. After all, Mark had run from her, too; and the *gentleness* with which Noah treated his kids—the hurt in his eyes, the shadows of the past—showed the man he was.

A man who wanted to be her friend. A man who *needed* a friend right now—and oh, she'd been there. Holding it all in, aching sometimes for just *one* person to understand…

*I can understand. I've been there—well, almost.*

So, they'd be friends. Right. She could do that.

She jumped the low fence and came to where he stood waiting for her, halfway up a grassy hill overlooking the sea. A deeper shade of darkness in the summer night; a man lost in the past.

The kicking of her pulse as she drew closer made a mockery of her thoughts on friendship.

It was obvious she'd have to be very careful. Noah Brannigan was more than a harassed single dad struggling to make things right in an impossible situation; he was far from the average man. He'd already shown he could see through the shutters covering her eyes to the pain she kept hidden beneath. If he saw the unwilling pull he held over her already…if he realised she'd spent an hour working out which of her shabby old sundresses to wear tonight—whether to replait her hair after she'd washed the paint out of it, or if it would look too obvious to wear it out.

So many years since she'd been through this kind of anticipatory torture; a lifetime since she'd *wanted* to think about it. Her life had been *safe*—then a man tapped on her back door, wanting his adorable, hurting kids back, and changed her world with a single smile.

"Hi."

Even his voice held power over her, as warm as the night, as dark as the gravel road leading to their houses. She was glad night concealed her blush. "Hi."

The darkness of his hand swept sideways. "There's a blanket there, if you can see it. I brought crackers and cheese, too. I hope you like white wine?"

"I do," she agreed cautiously, hoping it wasn't *very* dry. "I don't like reds."

"Lucky pick, then." A soft chuckle filled the air. "Hold on." With a click, the soft light of a double-halogen camping lantern blurred the darkness, and she could see his face. "I was saving the batteries until you came. I have mosquito repellent as well."

She watched him light the coil, wondering how she could be absorbed by so simple a thing. How could he make her tremble without touching her, or even looking at her? "Please, get comfortable," was all he said.

She sank down onto the rug, and opened the small basket. "A night-time picnic. I've never had this experience," she said, knowing she was babbling but unable to stop it.

"It's not much."

Sensing his embarrassment beneath the neutral tone, she relaxed and smiled up at him. "It's the experience that counts, not what you eat." She waved a hand heavenward. "Look at it, Noah." Wanting to say his name for no reason she could discern; just wanting to. "The clear, clean sky, the stars. The sound of the ocean, the smell of the grass. Wine and cheese."

"And thee. It's almost poetic." With a grin, he sat down facing her. "Are you always so positive?"

She chuckled. "I know, it's annoying. My—" she hesitated before she said it "—my ex-husband used to call me Pollyanna." *And not in an admiring way, either.*

Noah relaxed with the reference to Mark, and she guessed he'd already known about the divorce. Henry the mechanic or June, the postmistress had passed on the gossip when they found out where he lived, no doubt. "Cynicism is everywhere these days. It gets old quickly. Don't underestimate simple happiness."

Touched, she smiled at him. "Thanks for inviting me tonight."

"Thanks for coming." He smiled back, turning her insides to warm jelly. "I love it out here at night, but it's good to have adult company. Don't get me wrong—I love my kids—but this hour of peace before bed…"

"You don't need to explain, I work with kids all day," she said, trying to laugh. "I usually sit on my back verandah for an hour about this time."

*Shut up, Jennifer. You're sounding breathless again. It's enough to send the man running.*

An awkward silence fell between them: two people trying to not try too hard. People who didn't know each other, yet had so much unspoken already. Strangers with far too many things to *not* say.

"You couldn't have had a worse introduction to my family," he said abruptly, when the silence became unbearable. "You and your uncle Joe both."

He was crumbling a cracker in his hand, it was so tense.

"Please." Acting on impulse, she laid a hand over his, stilling the movement. "You must have seen how much I enjoyed playing with the kids today, and as for Uncle Joe—" she grinned then "—Tim's turning up there was almost inspired. He adores having anyone visit his junkyard, let alone a boy totally fascinated by all the rusty rubbish he's got there. Tim made his day by asking all those questions. Uncle Joe said he was welcome back any time—and he meant every word."

Instead of relaxing with the reassurance, Noah shrugged. "I guess I'll know where to find him from now on, at least."

"Is that so bad?" she asked gently, hearing the underlying grimness in the words.

He poured wine into two glasses. "So long as he doesn't bother your uncle, I suppose it's all right."

She sensed that wasn't what Noah wanted to say, but after her gaffe this afternoon, she knew better than to push the issue. "Uncle Joe's been pretty lonely since Aunty Jean died two years ago, and my cousins all moved to Sydney or Brisbane for work. He doesn't see his own grandchildren more than twice a year—and though I visit him every week, I'm not a junkyard kind of girl," she laughed. "I suspect Tim's about to be adopted."

"I suspect he'll love it. A million places to hide."

"But always safe," she said softly, trying to soften whatever hardness lay beneath the light words. Wanting to heal the festering hurt so deep inside him, even though she knew she couldn't. "Uncle Joe will make sure he won't hurt himself."

As if he sensed her anxiety, Noah smiled at her. "True." He handed her a glass of wine. "Have you always run day-care centres?"

Willing to follow his lead—and wanting to talk of things other than the kids he loved dearly yet worried him so much—she nodded. "I did my diploma straight out of high school, then went for the full degree by correspondence while doing a nursing degree. I also keep up my Advanced First Aid. I always planned to open my own place—but with rental and insurance, let alone hiring staff, it was more than I could afford in the Newcastle area."

Ah, so that was where she was from? Noah had wondered—she seemed to be so much a *part* of this place. "Is that where you grew up?"

"Yes. A born and bred Novocastrian—my parents still live in Swansea, by the ocean."

"My parents still live out west of Dural in Sydney," he said abruptly, almost adding, *so did Belinda's parents.* He and Belinda had started school together, grown up on the same street and had been together from the age of fifteen.

He didn't want to think about Belinda—it was like running on a treadmill, exhausting him and ultimately, going nowhere. "They're travelling around the country now, though. How many kids do you have every day?"

*And why don't you have any kids of your own?*

"I have three to four children each day, usually. I have a licence for up to six kids, but since I work alone, I won't over-burden myself. Not that there's many kids in Hinchliff who have working mothers who need me to give full-time care." She laughed again, the sound sweet and clear in the late summer night.

The aura of summer shimmered in the air around her. She was like the tiny purple star-flowers blossoming amid the warm grass waving in the wind: unexpected and lovely. A piece of old-fashioned prettiness dotting the uniformity of unending blades of grass that was his life.

Watching her walking to him in the thin white dress, her plait falling over one shoulder, she'd seemed the embodiment of a country night. She'd seemed to float toward him rather than walk in the soft moonglow, glimmering like a gentle beacon.

And he still wanted her. He wanted to hover around her aura like a lost moth, to slip inside it and feel her contentment and quiet joy in life. He wanted to sit here and drink in her face, to keep *feeling* her hand on his and this time, not let go...

Pulling away was too damn hard at this moment. It had been too long since he'd felt the night-heat of a woman's touch—a woman who wanted him, too.

And she did. It was in those soft blue eyes of hers, in the curve of her mouth...in the way she leaned into his lightest touch. In the breathlessness of her words when he was close to her, and the slight tremble when they touched. It was in the dress she wore, and the soft vanilla scent on her skin, a perfume she hadn't been wearing when they'd met. In the tendrils of loose hair escaped from her plait, half-curling around her face. In the gloss on her lips—lips she kept wetting with her tongue when she looked at him.

Jennifer wanted him, too—so much she didn't even seem to know how to hide it.

It couldn't happen. He wouldn't let it. The last thing he needed was the demands of a relationship, and the last thing his kids could cope with was a new mother-figure in their lives—especially Tim.

But even though flirting with danger was wrong, stupid, still he did it. Turning his hand beneath hers, not lifting or threading his fingers through hers, but feeling the soft warmth of palm to palm. "So you came here to start your business?"

Her gaze dropped to where their hands weren't quite linked—and slowly, her fingers moved; just a fraction, the tiniest, most tentative caress he'd ever known. Terrified and sweet, it acted on him like he'd downed the whole bottle of wine at a gulp.

As did her soft, breathless voice, saying all her words didn't. "I needed a fresh start after Mark and I divorced. Uncle Joe needed family close by—he's well physically and fine mentally, but he's getting older, you know? I came to visit, saw an opportunity since there was no other day-care providers here and ended up staying."

It took him almost a minute to work out what he'd asked, what she'd said in reply. He was too lost in the newfound wonder. His mind was caught up in the beating of his pounding pulse, in the sudden rush of hot wanting. She'd moistened her lips again. Her gaze fluttered down to his mouth, then back to his eyes, with a fugitive feminine shyness that left him drunk on need.

He had no experience in coping with this sudden rush of hot wanting; he'd never been with any woman but Belinda. Though he'd had the years of flirting and parties, it'd all revolved around Belinda; he didn't know how to play the game with a new woman.

He didn't think Jennifer knew how, either.

Both of them sat there, two feet apart, hands barely touching. Bowled over by this slamming of want and neither one knowing what to do with it—

Who was he fooling? They both knew what they wanted to do…it was the *consequences* of giving in to the desire they didn't know how to handle.

"What do you do with your life? Besides bringing up your kids?" Her voice held the aching femininity of a woman's desire.

He forced words from a closed-up throat. "I'm an architect and builder. I had a business in Sydney—the whole home-building package from start to finish." He didn't add that he'd had to sell off the Sydney business to pay off debts. It wasn't Belinda's fault—he ought to have seen her suffering. But lost in building up the business, then maintaining its prestige and success, he'd relied on Belinda's strength to keep the home-front going smoothly. He'd noticed she was buying a lot more things, sure, but they were doing well—why shouldn't she enjoy it? And if their married life had lost its intimacy since a few months before Rowdy's birth, he'd thought time and patience would fix it.

The full extent of her problems had only burst on him after she'd disappeared…and when the demands for payment had come, one after the other, from dresses and shoes to Internet gaming sites.

Jennifer's laugh burst in on his thoughts, feminine, unsteady, *wanting*. "And you moved to *Hinchliff?* What will you do in a town with two thousand residents?"

Glad to be diverted, he grinned. "Yeah, not that many opportunities for that kind of work here—so I thought I'd start up a renovation business. I'll be offering designs to suit any type of extension, for any era of house. And I could still offer new building services as well. There are a few new estates going up on the highway north and south of Ballina. That's not too far from here." He hesitated, knowing what he needed to say, to ask, but hating to put it on her. Still feeling the warmth of their semi-linked hands bringing him to life, touching a part of him he'd thought dead until a week ago. Until he'd seen Jennifer. "Of course, with Cilla and Rowdy too young yet for school, I'll only work part-time during the day. I can design at night."

Her eyes thoughtful, she nodded. "I—" Her hesitation was as obvious, as strong as his. "I have places for them both in day-care on Monday, Wednesday and Fridays if you need that? I run the centre until six at night, so if you need to work back, Tim's more than welcome to come over those days after school, as well."

Contact established; danger signs put on the tracks and they were running on a line heading for a broken track over a cliff. He knew it; she knew it; and still they plunged ahead.

After a short silence, she rushed on, her voice uneven. She pulled her hand from his, showing her nervousness—and no wonder, with the amount of times he'd shut her out today. "It'd be a business arrangement of course. I—I only have three kids on those days…and I don't charge that much…"

"Jennifer." To his surprise, he'd already laid his hand back over hers. "Thank you. I was hoping you'd have space. It's hard dragging the kids everywhere, as I had to in Sydney— and as for Tim—" He sighed. "I think he'd like it—especially if I'm not there to complicate things."

"I think it was me who complicated things," she said quietly, looking down at her lap, but she didn't move her hand from beneath his.

"We both complicated it," he admitted, just as quiet.

The wanting, the desire all but shimmered between them, and they were barely touching.

She looked up. "I think it's best for Tim if I go back home. I think we both have enough ghosts to deal with."

Aching to touch his lips to the curve of her neck, or to the exposed shoulder just beneath him….to lift her face to his— all he could do was nod. He knew she was right, but hearing the words filled him with resentment. He *wanted* Jennifer, damn it—just as she wanted him; but he was barred from the normal male-female attraction games, because of this damned *limbo*. Would he never stop paying the price for a few months of emotional blindness?

*Am I giving Tim security and stability by being alone, or bowing to an insecure child's demands, and making things worse for the whole family? Cilla and Rowdy need a mother figure in their lives...and Tim needs it more than both of them together.*

Why had he never thought of that before?

"I'd better go," she whispered, but she still didn't move her hand.

*"Daddy!"*

Noah scrambled to his feet. "It's Tim," he said tersely.

*"Daddy! Daddy!"*

He bolted to the house, through the kitchen and down the hall in to the big, blue room Tim shared with Rowdy. Even though it was a four-bedroom house, Tim didn't like sleeping alone. Though he'd never admit it, his baby brother's presence, his tiny snores and the comfort of Rowdy's *Sesame Street* posters and baby mobiles and teddy bears gave him a sense of continuity and safety. "It's okay, matey, I'm here."

He lifted his sobbing son into his arms, holding him close: the only time Tim would allow Noah into his space. He whispered inane words of comfort, caressing Tim's spiky shock of streaky hair, his palm wet with the sweat drenching his child. Tim was shivering, wracked with the terror again. Noah held him and rocked him, realising anew why he lived alone. Aching for the pain that never went away, locked inside a father's anguish that made him want to promise anything to make his little boy better, if only for a few hours.

"Daddy," he mumbled, lost in a world between sleeping, waking and the fear that walked with him night and day. The fear that separated him from all the other kids at school, made him different, because nobody else's mummy had *disappeared*. If Belinda had died, Tim would have accepted it by now, moved on and begun to heal; but there was nowhere to go when your mother was a missing person. There was no end, no closure or healing, just unending pain and the terror that it was your fault she didn't want to come home.

It was a burden too heavy for any little boy to carry around and still be normal.

"I'm here, matey. I'll always be here," he swore now to his son, wishing it didn't feel like a damned lie—that Tim could believe it. But he didn't and Noah didn't: the fragility of life and belonging was a lesson burned onto their skins with a branding iron.

Promises were something too easily broken. Belinda had proven that.

"Make her go away, Daddy..." Tim buried his face in Noah's shoulder, heaving with sobs too hacking to be an act to get his way.

Noah sighed, knowing this time, it was a promise he couldn't make. "I can't, matey," he whispered back, throat thick with pain as he kissed Tim's forehead. "She's our neighbour—and she'll be minding Cilla and Rowdy while I work."

The hiccups came thick and fast. "No, Daddy," Tim sobbed. "Mummy will never come home if—if..."

Tim couldn't even say it, couldn't finish the words.

Noah ached and burned with guilt piling on guilt, because this time he couldn't say he didn't want or like the woman who was threatening Tim's peace of mind. No matter how hard he tried, he couldn't lie to his son about this—because he *did* want Jennifer, and it would show every time he saw her. He wanted her even now, when he should be resenting her intrusion into his mind and body at the worst possible time.

Worst of all, he *liked* her—and this time Tim knew the danger was real. With his radar tuned in to his father day and night, needing him as much as he punished him, he'd sensed the danger even before Noah had.

There was nothing he could say to reassure his son, and the nightmares, the fear, would just go on and on.

Some instinct alerted him. He turned his head.

Jennifer stood in the doorway, her face white, eyes glistening with the tears spilling over in silence. A shaking hand, fisted tight, covered her mouth as she looked at Tim.

Slowly she lifted her gaze to Noah. He couldn't move, couldn't breathe. He could feel her driving need to reach out, to help them both—but if she did, Tim would know they'd been together, and he'd never feel safe again.

There was nothing she could do to help this, nothing she could say. It was over before it began. For half an hour they'd reached out to the fire—now it was burning an innocent child.

Without a sound she vanished, leaving only sadness and regret in her wake.

Jennifer was sitting on the picnic blanket, downing her second glass of wine when he came back. He stopped a few feet from her. Waiting for an explanation as to why she was still there.

Feeling like a complete idiot—why *hadn't* she gone home, instead of sitting here drinking his wine?—she said, sounding lame even to her ears, "Is—is he all right now?"

"No." A terse word. "He's in my bed. I just came out to pack up the picnic before wild mice get to it."

"I'll do it." She scrambled off the blanket.

"No, Jennifer. Please, just go," he said quietly. "If he wakes up and comes out—"

She nodded, feeling even worse, if it were possible. "I just needed to know he was—"

So awkward, all these silences. Saying everything but the things they needed to say.

"He won't be all right until Belinda comes back…or her body's found." He went on, the words bursting from him.

"It's not like a death. That's bad enough. But *this* is like permanent purgatory. The pieces of my life are jagged, and they keep cutting me—and cutting Tim, Cilla and Rowdy— over and over." He swiped a hand across his face, as if pushing the intensity and despair from his features. "There's nowhere to go, no way to move on. In Tim's mind, healing is disloyalty—even moving here feels to him like I've accepted her death. How do I tell him he's wrong to keep hoping, to keep looking for her in every car, bus or train? How do I say 'it's not Mummy' every time the phone rings and he runs for it? What if Belinda *is* alive and comes back? I know he's told Cilla that, too, so she feels the same even though she can't remember Belinda. Rowdy just doesn't understand. So we just exist, waiting for her, waiting for news—for anything that gives us permission to live without this damned hope and fear and *guilt* eating us all alive."

There was nothing more useless than unwanted tears. She gulped them back, but oh, how she *wanted* to wrap her arms around him right now, to let him know he didn't have to be so alone with all this pain…that she understood more than he knew.

But touching him was taboo, and her fascinated stare must be embarrassing him.

Jennifer closed her eyes against the force of this beautiful, tortured man. "I should have gone home. I'm sorry…I was worried."

"By now you must be worrying you're living next door to a basket case. I'm sorry, Jennifer." Another weary swipe of his hand over his face. "It might be a relief for me to talk, but you don't need to hear it."

"Maybe you needed to say it," she said quietly, giving him what she could. Unable to reach out because of a simple truth: she was utterly fascinated by this man, and touching him, even in comfort, was too dangerous. "And maybe saying it to a stranger felt cleansing."

"Maybe, but you're not a stranger," he muttered, his eyes intense on her.

Slowly she nodded. Accepting the rebuke, and the danger, without his speaking of either. They weren't strangers—but they couldn't be anything more than that.

"Jennifer."

Slowly she looked up, compelled by the starkness in his voice. Those jagged pieces of his life were ripping at him again. She knew—oh, how she *knew*...

He didn't look at her. His whole attention seemed focussed on packing up the little basket. "Even if Belinda's dead—and I believe she is—I have nothing left to give. You probably can't understand..."

Hearing the words *hurt,* even if she'd known it before she'd even seen him. Even if she knew all the reasons why she, too, had so little to give. Why she might take a lover, but never a husband—and as her life with Cody had been, Noah's life didn't allow for brief flings.

"To have a child you can't kiss better, you can't heal no matter how hard you try, kills you piece by piece," she said softly, "but you can't stop hoping, can't stop trying. You have no choice but to put them first—even when you worry you're spoiling them or making a rod for your back later." She smiled and shrugged, and before he could ask her how she knew so much, she handed him the picnic blanket she hadn't even known she was folding, and turned away. "Bring Cilla and Rowdy over whenever you need to work. Doesn't matter what days, okay? No notice needed."

"Jennifer..." In the darkness, a hand—that sturdy, dependable brown hand—reached out to her, and she ached to touch him one final time.

A wave crashed below them. The tide was right in, attacking the sandstone walls below them. It was a lonely sound.

She shook her head, trying to smile. "Best not to."

His gaze was deep and intense. "I can't do all the taking. It's not in me."

"You aren't," she assured him quietly. "You're paying me. I'm saving money to have my verandah rebuilt bigger, and get a new cubby house for the kids, a portable one." She flushed as she said it, though why, she had no idea. "I've been thinking of selling up and moving into town—it'll be closer for the kids…well, most of them…"

"We both know you're still the one giving the most in this arrangement." His voice was grim. "So I'll design and build your verandah and cubby house for you. Just pay for the materials. No charge for labour, not while you're minding the kids. I need to start up my business again, heaven knows—" he didn't even crack a smile as he said it "—and it can serve as local advertising at the same time."

She heard the prickly note in his voice. She couldn't find it in her to blame him; his day would reach any sane man's limits. "If it serves us both, all I can say is thank you, Noah."

"Good." Only then did he smile—and it was as if he'd cracked apart the wall of isolation she'd been trying to build. "If I get some really big work in the interim—"

Knowing what he couldn't say, she nodded. "Of course, you have a family to support. To finish up before and after work will be fine. The kids are still with you then. We can alternate dinners, maybe. One night I cook, another you can bring it home."

"Thank you, Jennifer. I don't know how to say…" His voice trailed off. Husky, but not with desire: rough with the gratitude of a man who'd carried his burdens alone too long.

And though she knew that, still she thought of what she couldn't have, and blushed. "I have to go. Good night, Noah."

*Pollyanna strikes again,* her inner voice taunted as she walked away without looking back.

She was setting herself up for a fall; it was as inevitable as the tide coming in below her feet. After two years of wandering through a half-dreaming existence, she was alive again—and it hurt. The worst part of it was until she could change the person she was, she had no choice in it. Within a day she knew Noah Brannigan had the power to destroy her, yet she couldn't do a thing about it without hurting his beautiful children, or making his suffering worse.

Heart against conscience, and the pull of needing children. No, she had no choice—and she knew whatever price she'd pay for her decision, she went into it with her eyes open.

She hoped.

# CHAPTER FOUR

*Six weeks later*

"JENNY! Jenny, we're here!"

As she sipped her morning coffee, she found herself smiling at Rowdy's enthusiastic interruption to her routine. Usually this was her quiet time before the other kids arrived, but Tim, Cilla and Rowdy weren't "other" kids. What it was about them that called her so strongly, she only wished she knew. She loved all the children she cared for but the Brannigans had broken through the eggshell-thin wall of self-protection around her heart. Perhaps it was because the family needed her so much.

No, the Brannigan *children* needed her. Noah only needed her child-minding skills.

Apart from the days she had the kids, he'd been over only twice in the past six weeks—to draw up the plans, and show them to her. He'd called to let her know the local council had approved the plans, and again to let her know he'd be starting work today.

He was cutting and assembling her new cubby house in his yard, and would bring it over when it was done. "I thought it'd be a joint project I could do with Tim," he'd told her in a gruff voice. She didn't know if the odd note was because he was using an excuse to avoid her—or because Tim was refusing to hammer in a single nail when his father was around.

He might not be running off quite so much—only twice since the night they'd met—but that didn't mean he wasn't going to keep punishing Noah for his invisible crimes.

She didn't flatter herself that it was *her* influence that stopped Tim running off. She only wished she knew what it was—

Rowdy erupted into the kitchen with a big, glowing smile, sure of his welcome. He ran straight into Jennifer's arms with all the confidence he'd shown from the first day. Knowing he was loved. "Jenny, I'm here! Are you happy?"

"Of course, very happy," Jennifer chuckled as she hugged him. He always stated the obvious, and asked the same thing every day. "Are you hungry?"

He nodded with vigour, though Jennifer was sure Noah would have fed all of them before coming over. "Toast and Vegemite!"

She hugged him again, and swung Cilla up onto her other hip, giving her a big kiss before she answered. "Sorry, sweetie, no can do. I have three other kids coming soon." Whenever she gave him the spread, it seemed to give him a massive burst of energetic chatter and climbing she couldn't cope with when she had other children to watch.

It was the only time he fulfilled the nickname Tim told her Noah had given him soon after his birth—the baby who constantly made noise. She often wondered if he'd quietened down by nature or necessity. Tim and Cilla needed so much more than he did…he seemed such a happy child, but she watched him, just in case.

As Tim walked through the door with far more caution than the other kids showed, she suggested, "How about baked beans and cheese on toast?"

That was Tim's favourite, but Rowdy tended to emulate

Tim—at least when Tim wasn't angry or screaming. Rowdy was perpetually good-natured.

Tim grinned and nodded. "Thanks," he said: a reluctant concession to manners, and as gruff as his father always was when he felt overwhelmed.

Cilla made a tiny sound.

Jennifer smiled down at Cilla, hiding the ball of emotion the non-request engendered. After six weeks of constant invitation, the little girl still didn't have the courage to ask for anything she wanted. "Chocolate spread and mashed banana for Cilla, of course."

The glowing smile was reward enough.

Noah knocked on the door, polite and withdrawn—the constant reminder of the wall between them. "Good morning, Jennifer."

"Good morning, Noah," she returned, grave and just as polite. Trying to smile as normal, but if she did, he'd smile back, and she'd forget what she was doing—and Tim would see it.

"I just made coffee. Would you like some?" she offered as he walked through to the little-used front door, and put barrier tape across it, in preparation for tearing out the front verandah.

He turned back from his task. "Yes, thank you."

It took all she had not to gulp—Tim was watching—but Noah's simple good manners made her feel as if she'd just endured three rounds with a kickboxing champion. She clung to the memory of their night together as dearly as if they'd made love: it was all she was likely to have. Remembering his rare smile, the way his hand turned beneath hers in a promise unspoken…

She put Cilla down after another gentle kiss, and got Rowdy into the high chair, strapping him in. "I'll just get the kids set first."

She turned away from the sight of him as if he was just another father dropping off his kids, or a tradesman working on her house. A crazy infatuation, an unrequited attraction.

So why did she always feel as if he'd touched her, when he never did? He hadn't touched her once, nor even come close to her, from that first night. Why was it he could break years of self-sufficiency and good sense with a look, or a smile—or even by the lack of them?

"Jen? Here's the baked beans." Noah's personal watchdog stood in front of her, waiting. Watching. On guard.

She blinked and smiled at Tim. "You're such a good help." She smiled down at the boy, feeling his hunger for the close-ness of touch, and his fear and loathing of it. Poor little man needed a mother so much, even more than Cilla and Rowdy did; but he barricaded himself from the simple joy of a hug because she was a woman, and therefore a threat to his security. His mother was no more than a distant memory; his vow was all he had left of Belinda.

With a sense of fatality she made the breakfast. Child-carer, just the child-carer...

That coffee was a long time coming.

Noah muttered words he'd never use in front of the kids as he tore up one plank after the other, glad for something heavy and physical to do. He'd work himself to exhaustion, if that's what it would take to quieten the screaming demands of his body, the whispers of his heart.

Every time he saw her now, her pretty face, her tenderness and unassuming grace filled him like the thrumming of a guitar chord, reverberating through every pore. Even just living within five hundred metres of her house, knowing she was there, made the masculine hunger roar to life. When he had to pick up the kids, to see her kissing his kids, caring for them, and yet to know, to feel the barriers neither could breach, he ached and burned.

At night he relived their one night out beneath the stars…the night where nothing, yet so much, seemed to have happened between them. Floating toward him in that white dress, soft half-curls escaping her plait. Just the joy of talking with her…seeing her hand over his; watching her smile at him, her eyes touched with desire…

Most nights he woke up in a sweat that had little to do with the current heatwave—on the nights Tim didn't wake him up with nightmares, at least. No wonder they were both short-tempered these days; neither of them were getting much sleep.

Tim rarely spoke to him now, but he kept watching.

He had no idea how Jennifer felt about him. She seemed so serene, treating him as if he was just another day-care daddy, offering coffee the same way she did to the mothers who dropped their kids here—or worse, like he was her uncle.

He swore as a massive splinter ripped through his thick glove and pierced his thumb.

"Noah?"

Hearing the concern in her voice, he reacted with brusque rejection. "I'm fine."

"Here's your coffee."

The gentle care had vanished; her words were neutral, almost too neutral. He looked up. Her smile was calm, determined. *She* would keep her manners; and it made him feel like a schoolboy being rebuked by his teacher, and just as foolish.

He put out a hand to take the cup, but she put it down beside him.

"Jennifer—" he started to apologise, disgusted by the husky note in his voice at using the name. The *neediness* just using her name provoked in him.

Wanting to touch her, if only for a moment. His temper igniting because there was no way he could take the risk.

He turned away. "I have some quotes to do today. I'll be out until Tim's back from school. Is it okay to work on the verandah from four until dark?"

"Of course." Her gaze moved to his gloved right hand, and the splinter sticking out from his thumb at an angle. "I'll get tweezers and antiseptic. I'll send them out with Tim."

"It has to be this way, Jennifer," he growled, hating the distance. *Hating it.*

She turned to look at him for a moment, her eyes not quite meeting his. "I'm not arguing." Then she sighed. "I have to go in. I asked Tim to mind the kids while I brought out the coffee, and it's interrupting his routine. He hasn't got much time before the school bus."

"He's ready for school."

She frowned and tilted her head.

"He's watching us through the glass of the front door," he said quietly.

She didn't make the mistake of looking. "Then he'll be re-assured, won't he?"

His left glove flicked away as he tossed it. Wishing he knew what she felt beneath the controlled words, he pulled the splinter from his glove. Wishing she'd go back inside before he did something really stupid.

"It's not just about you and Tim, you know."

The sudden intensity of it took him aback. He looked up again. She stood over him, her fists curled, and a strand of half-curl dancing across her face in the hot morning wind—and so pretty with her cheeks flushed and her eyes flashing with anger. He ached to brush that strand away: it was that bad with him now, just touching her hair would be enough—and he was a whisper away from *really, really stupid* now.

"What is it, then?" He winced at the harsh question: such a pitiful mask for the craving.

As if she'd felt the almost violent need in him, she brushed the lock of hair away, but it came dancing back within moments. She tugged it back hard behind one ear. "You don't need to know. You're just the father of three kids I happen to have fallen madly in love with."

*Wham.*

Just like that, his belief in shared sleepless nights, angst and craving shattered. She'd only spoken truth as she saw it; not how she felt or what she wanted, but what *was*. Why the truth made everything she'd awoken in him rise up in hot rebellion, he didn't know, but he was on his feet, striding toward her without thought, ready to haul her against him and prove she was lying.

A movement by the window stopped him cold.

"Then why say anything, if you weren't going to tell me?" he snapped, not knowing who or what he was most furious about. He'd bricked them inside four walls together, separated by a wall of Perspex neither could batter down.

One brow lifted as she contemplated his anger and obvious frustration. "So you'll stop apologising. I have good reasons why there will never be another man in my life. I won't bother you." She turned her head away, but not before he saw the flash of want in her eyes. "You don't need to worry I'll jump on you. I wouldn't make a fool of myself."

*Won't bother him?* She did that just by being here, so close, so lovely, so graceful and so tempting…talking about *jumping on him*. Everything about her bothered him to insanity point.

"My bus will be here in a minute."

Tim made his announcement through the window beside the taped-off door. Noah cursed his stupidity; Tim must have heard everything they'd said. Why hadn't he taped the window shut, as well? He could have sworn he had.

A swift glance showed that Tim had slowly peeled the tape away and opened the window to listen in on them.

"Re-tape the window, please, Tim," he said coolly, asserting authority. "And don't peel it back again. You could put the day-care kids in danger if my work isn't taped and roped off from Jennifer's business. If you want to listen to our conversations, come outside and do it honestly."

"Yes, Dad." Tim didn't so much as look at his father, but his voice was filled with trust as he turned back to Jennifer. It was a trust she'd earned with cooking lessons and games of paintbrush wars, his favourite food—and never looking at Noah as if she wanted him. "The kids are watching *Sesame Street,* Jen, so can I go?"

"Of course, Tim. Thanks for your help."

Her voice was just as warm as Tim's. The mutual admiration society had just upped a notch, thanks to Jennifer's blunt statement that she'd never pursue Tim's only security. Tim liked Jennifer; Cilla and Rowdy adored her, and she loved them all.

He was the only one locked out.

He couldn't look at her anymore. Life was too hard as it was. He didn't need the answer, as logical as it was impossible, standing right in front of him, reminding him of everything he couldn't have. "Don't bother with the tweezers. I got the splinter myself. Thanks."

There was no way she could miss the freezing politeness in his voice.

She didn't answer, but the rustling of hot air touching his face told him she was gone.

"Oh, good grief," Jacey's mother Kate muttered the next afternoon, as she stared out the back window. She was the last mother for the day, and she, like the others, married or single, had done the same thing.

Stared at Noah as if he was manna fallen from heaven…

In the light of the setting sun he was tearing up old wooden slats and tossing them behind him. He was wearing only cutoff jeans and work boots; his bare, tanned chest and builder's strong arms were slick with sweat; his legs were muscular and brown. His hair took on the sun's glow, touched at its ends with golden fire.

"Jen, you lucky, lucky girl," Kate muttered, drinking in the sight Jennifer had been studiously avoiding for the past hour. "How on earth do you live next door to *that,* have him here day and night and *not* get into the horizontal tango with that gorgeous man?"

"Shhh," Jennifer whispered frantically, with a quick glance back to where Tim watched a re-run of something, Jacey on his lap, and Cilla and Rowdy played a game of memory cards.

Kate grinned, impudent and unashamed. "Come on, girl, are you dead? Lost your hormones? Coz otherwise you can't tell me you don't spend hours every day looking, and itching." She lifted a brow in cheeky suggestion. "Make me coffee and tell me all. I swear if I wasn't happy with Nick…"

How many more times would she hear the same thing? It wasn't as if her rebel body needed the encouragement!

After she'd eventually ushered Kate and Jacey out of the house, Jennifer sighed. Why couldn't she find the words to shut the mouths of the curious and determined? It was bad enough that every child's mother had asked the same thing, and her mother, alerted by Uncle Joe, was calling from Italy for updates; her quilting friends Veronica and Jessie had also met him when Tim took off last week, and Noah had come over looking for his son. Wearing only a singlet top and denim shorts, his body gleaming with sweat from making her cubby house…

Not one person in town believed they weren't lovers. Not

one person didn't fill her imagination daily with visions she couldn't lock out of her head.

Not with him *there,* looking like that…

Like Kate, like Annie and Olga and every other woman with a beating heart and hormones, Jennifer was mesmerised. Through the elusive, shifting colours of her old stained window, he seemed godlike, a glowing being of strength and power…and a rich male beauty that left her breathless and hurting.

Trying to behave, she'd done no more than steal glances as the kids played and she stitched her latest quilt she was making; yet every peek made her feel like a sneak thief in her own home. But she was helpless to stop herself from doing it, over and over.

Quilting was a form of creation she could take anywhere, one she'd learned at the Children's Hospital during Cody's stays. It kept her hands busy and her mind calm and centred, especially when she was tired or feeling negative.

Unless there happened to be exquisite, golden-brown temptation working just outside her window, bending down over lumber, wearing only hugging jeans…

She had to stop it, now!

Sticking the needle into the quilt, she folded it up and put it out of the reach of little hands. "Let's play a game of hide-and-seek before dark," she announced to the kids.

"Yeah!" Rowdy and Cilla bolted from the game of Memory they were playing, straight out the back door to the yard.

She looked at Tim, still watching some rerun of funny videos, with a smile she made deliberately impish. She couldn't show him that she'd suggested the game for his sake alone. Desperately hoping that, by playing the game so often, she could desensitise the issue of his disappearances whenever life overwhelmed him. "If you stay there I'm going to find you pretty fast, Tim—and Rowdy will crow about it all night."

With a chuckle, Tim ran for the back door.

After a slow, loud count to twenty, she walked out the back door after them, calling, "I'm coming to get you," in a way that never failed to make Rowdy giggle.

She always made sure Tim or Cilla won. Rowdy didn't seem to mind; he liked finishing the search with her, and once he'd said, "Timmy likes to win," for which she was awed. That a three-year-old had such self-esteem, and such insight into his insecure brother's needs, was a testament to Noah's rearing of his kids. That Tim and Cilla were healing so quickly—and they were—could only be laid at Noah's door, as well. All her training told her it should take far longer to have gained the kids' trust, and for them to let her in.

It amazed her that Noah didn't realise what a magnificent father he was.

"I'm coming to get you," she cried again, and heard the giggle from around the front of the house. Smiling, she called it over and over, hearing the laughter smothered by a hand, but still constant. Running around the old cubby at the side, she dashed into Rowdy's favourite hidey-haunt: behind the gardenia bushes at the front corner of the house. She dived on him, tickling his tummy. "Got you, bud!"

Rowdy shrieked with laughter, not in the least put out at being found first. "Let's get 'em, Jenny," he whispered very loudly, slipping his hand into hers.

Resisting the urge to kiss the little hand, she circled the yard at a little-kid running pace, crying out, "We're coming to get you!"

As they approached where Noah was tearing down her verandah, he turned his head: the golden-rose rays of sunset fell on his face as he smiled at them.

Jennifer lost her breath—and caught her toe. She tripped over a root and stumbled. Acting with lightning instinct, she twisted Rowdy so he came down on top of her as she fell to the spongy grass.

Seeming unhurt, he cackled with laughter. "We playing Ring Around the Rosie?"

"No," she laughed back, "Jenny's just playing dropsies."

"I thought *I* was the dropsy one around here."

His voice was close. *He* was close…too close. She turned her head, with the vestiges of laughter still in her eyes, to see him smiling down at them. "No." The word came out half-strangled. "I—why do you think I work with kids? I thought I'd put the family's genetic clumsiness to a good use. It entertains the kids no end."

Grinning, he put out his hands to them. "This feels like déjà vu." He lifted her to her feet. "But there are no pots to take off you this time."

*And no shirt, either.*

On her feet, Jennifer found herself in direct eye contact with his naked, brown chest; her hands, released from his, were a bare inch from touching him. He smelled like earth and grass and wood, and hardworking, raw, sensual male. His bare skin gleamed with honest sweat.

Heart racing, breathless, she didn't dare look up at him. She'd only make a fool of herself if she did…but she couldn't help it, couldn't stop it. Within moments her gaze lifted to his.

Deep, hot, strangely vulnerable as he took in the desire she couldn't hide…and *tender.* Will against wanting, need against reason…the aching current arced between them, impossible and beautiful—and her hands, with a will of their own, lifted that inch—

"We go finding Timmy and Cilla now?"

The hopeful question roused her from the lovely stupor. She shook her head to clear it, and her hands fell. She couldn't breathe, or speak with any semblance of normality. It was all she could do to smile down at Rowdy and nod.

Noah stepped back without a word, but a tiny smile hovered around his mouth.

On legs that felt like jelly, she took Rowdy's hand again, and headed toward the other side of the house.

And Noah, as off-kilter and damned scared as he knew Jennifer had been, turned back to the verandah, thanking heaven Tim hadn't seen that moment, for once. Thanking heaven for Rowdy's intervention, or he'd have taken her into his arms then and there…

He'd have to work himself into insensibility the next few hours. It was the only way he'd get any sleep tonight.

## CHAPTER FIVE

Tim came into the house without his usual passive-aggressive behaviour that disrupted the family—and Noah knew what he was going to say before he said it. "Dad, you got one of those big letters again."

The kids always left him alone to read them. They knew better than to get him going on "big letter" days—they just didn't know what the letters were or why they got to him.

He carried the letter into the kitchen, got a beer out and sat at the table. He knew he'd need it. Phone calls were positive news, a lead or a sighting of Belinda; a letter was always bad.

Dear Mr Brannigan,

It is with regret that I inform you we found the woman in question, and there is no possible way she could be your wife. Her name is Sandra Langtry, and she lives in a bush cabin in Broadwater National Park with her family. She has lived an alternative lifestyle for eighteen years and has given birth to four children in the past twelve years…

The words blurred in front of his eyes.

It was over. The only good sighting in the past eighteen months, and it led to nothing.

He downed the beer in seconds, but it did nothing; no amount of alcohol could douse the pain, the feeling that a chapter of his life should be closed, but the jagged shards of his life remained in the doorway, leaving it open. The cold winds of uncertainty and abandonment, the feeling of being stuck down a dark well he couldn't climb out of, filled him again.

Unless he did something about it; he had to take charge.

Closing off the door to the kitchen, he picked up the phone to make the call he'd been putting off for more than a year.

*A week later*

She had to stop looking. It was bordering on perversion, the way she kept finding reasons to sit here near this window, or looking every time he passed.

Which was *way* too often.

Dear God, the man was beautiful…like a statue of David come to warm, touchable flesh…

Would this mid-autumn heatwave never end? It'd been nine days now; nine days of endless heat, where Noah pulled his shirt off to work in the early evenings.

If only he'd keep his shirt on, she wouldn't be so—so lost in the sight of him all the time. Lost in the sight of warm golden-brown skin, muscle rippling beneath; lost in the smiles he gave her when he caught her looking. She was beyond counting the amount of stubbed toes or bruises on her legs from walking into things, or tripping over when she stared at him, but she knew she had fifty-two needle pricks in her index finger…

*Ouch.* Make that fifty-three.

Right. Stop it immediately. Lower gaze and look at your quilt before it's completely unsaleable. Yes, you can do that.

Her gaze lifted again within two minutes. Obviously self-control was not the forte she'd thought it was.

So Plan B: get out of the line of fire.

"I'm going out to the rocking chair," she announced to the kids. Yes, that was safe—the rocking chair was on the untouched side of the verandah, on the other side of the house from Noah. Take the kids, even better. A refuge against temptation. "Want to put on the hose and cool down on the Slip and Slide before I make dinner?"

During summer she took the kids to the beach, while it was patrolled, but the lifesavers packed up in late March, and she wasn't a strong enough swimmer to risk taking the children there alone. So they'd played on the wet mat every afternoon during the late-April heatwave, cooling down in the burning hour before sundown. Tim especially liked it when all the kids were there, and he was the big one who watched over them and made sure they were all safe.

"Yeah, Slip and Slide!" Rowdy would have run straight out if she hadn't stopped him, putting on his sunscreen shirt and hat. It might be late afternoon, but in heat like this his fair skin would burn.

When the kids were dressed and sunscreen applied, she let them bolt to the back door, and out. She followed, carrying her quilting basket. "Tim, don't forget to wet the whole slide first," she called, knowing Tim would, but he liked to hear again that he was the senior one, and he had the responsibility.

Tim was already hosing it down, his tongue sticking out with concentration. "No, Rowdy, you could hurt yourself," he said, waving his little brother back. "It'll be ready in a minute."

"Okay, Timmy—hurry." Rowdy stepped back and hopped from one foot to the other in impatient obedience.

As she patched in a small piece of curved rag to the main quilt, Jennifer smiled, watching the brothers. Tim was becoming a child of his family again; the past few weeks, he'd stopped running away, and seemed to begin accepting life here.

It had surprised her at first, given the depth of his anger and rebellion against Noah at the start; but if it worked, if his father thought the change was positive, who was she to question it?

If she saw something in Tim's eyes, in the way he spoke, and how he'd become a big brother again instead of verbally attacking Cilla and Rowdy that made her wonder, she could think of no reason for it. Nothing out of the ordinary had happened to bring about the change that she could think of.

"Maybe it's school?"

"What is?"

"Ouch!" She removed the needle, and rubbed at her jabbed finger. "Fifty-four," she muttered, glaring up at Noah—

*Would he never put his shirt back on?*

"Fifty-four what?" He looked down at her abused finger. "Sorry." He frowned, taking in the amount of pinprick jabs there. "Are you diabetic?"

"No." Embarrassed, she shrugged. "Just clumsy."

"And you chose quilting as your hobby? Did you see it as a challenge?" He chuckled and sat on the rocker next to her. "Why don't you get a thimble?"

"I've had a dozen—I keep losing them." She grinned back. "Quilting was an exercise in patience more than anything at first—a way to pass the hours. Before I knew it, I loved it. I've met a lot of my closest friends up here in the quilting circle."

"It looks very peaceful. Like you," he said quietly. Then he gulped down the tall glass of iced water he'd brought out with him.

The past week or more, he'd been making more of an effort to speak to her, to begin the friendship they'd spoken of the first night. They talked of their childhood, schooling, what made them choose their career paths. They talked of family still living, his brother, her sisters and brother and cousins. She told him about her parents travelling the world in their early retirement, as his parents were travelling around Australia in a campervan. They were currently in Western Australia, discovering the wildest northwest Outback.

It was so good to have an adult to speak to about something other than their children, but if there was two things she was certain of, it was that she couldn't be Noah's friend…and she was far from *peaceful.* Not when something as simple as watching him drink made her heart thunder and her breath seize in her lungs…watching the movement of his throat and small trickles of sweat run down the golden-brown skin…

*Fifty-five.*

She was quite proud of the fact that she didn't say "ouch" aloud this time.

"That's a nice quilt," he remarked, looking down at it. "It's nice and soft, with all those swirly bits in different shades of brown. What's the pattern? It looks like the spirit of autumn."

"I—" Oh, help, she hardly knew. This quilt had become her refuge from staring at him the past two weeks; she'd chosen colours and pattern at random.

Looking down, she took in what her fingers had been creating the past fortnight—and felt the heat flaring on her face. Double circles intertwining…golden-hearted rose petals…

She rushed into speech, before he asked another question. "It's…um, a traditional pattern, popular since the early twentieth century—and—and since it's autumn…"

*Babbling again,* she thought in disgust. If any other of her quilting club were here, they'd give her a knowing grin and tease her unmercifully about her Freudian slip. It was a wonder they hadn't noticed it at the Friday night "eat-fest."

It was a traditional pattern, all right, and very popular: a wedding quilt. And what was worse, it was all in the colours of maple and caramel and golden-brown—autumn shades, but also the colours of Noah's eyes and hair and skin.

She hadn't even known until now, when the evidence was right in front of her; but she couldn't deny her unconscious desires, revealed by her creation.

Lust she could handle; she had been, barring a few physical injuries—try a few hundred—but if she was dreaming of everything—of the marriage and babies she couldn't risk—

*Come on, Pollyanna, fix this one,* she heard a voice taunting her. *What man will want a tainted strain he can't even have kids with?*

*Noah already has children. He doesn't need a baby from you,* her mind whispered.

*But that's not the real problem,* she admitted wearily to herself.

All her life she'd wanted just one thing: to be a wife and mother. To be rounded with her babies, feeling them kick, to feed at her breast, reading stories to her children, singing songs. The whole nine yards that went with it, even the hours of worrying about teenagers let off the leash.

Well, she'd had it—and Cody had been the one to pay the price for her dreams.

"Jennifer? Are you okay? Is the heat getting to you?"

When he spoke like that, touched with caring, his voice ran over her with rough sweetness, making her forget everything: the past, her pain—everything but the rush of wanting him.

*You can't have him. No touching.*

She gulped and blurted out, "I should ask you that question, since you've always got your shirt off these days. I wish you'd put it back on—then I wouldn't have all these injur—" She skidded to a horrified halt, her mouth open to speak and she couldn't seem to close it.

Terrified but unable to stop it, she looked up at him.

He was biting the inside of his lip, but it didn't quite cover the grin. His eyes were warm with laughter and something deeper, hotter and infinitely more masculine. "I didn't realise it was bothering you. I'll keep it on, then."

She had to force her mouth closed, to stop the protest coming out. Now she'd gotten what she'd needed the past couple of weeks, she wished she'd just kept her silly mouth shut.

Nothing short of sudden blindness would stop her staring at him, anyway.

A trickle of sweat ran down her neck. God help her, she was so obvious it was pitiful! She jumped to her feet, letting the quilt apparatus scatter across the verandah. "Make way, kids!" she hollered, and bolted for the Slip and Slide.

The kids laughed and scattered for her, knowing when she gave that war whoop, she was going for it—a full-on slide all the way down...

Picking up her quilting stuff, Noah watched her run and slide to her hip as she landed on the wet length of plastic, her legs in the air, with absolutely no grace or dignity. He hid a knowing grin. She might be having fun now, but he knew why she'd needed to cool down; and while he couldn't do a thing about that particular heat, the man in him loved his power over her.

The same power she held over him.

Strange, but though he'd always thought her pretty, at first it was in a more ordinary way: the same kind of appreciation he had for the flowers in her garden. They were lovely, but something he could see anywhere. He wanted her; she'd woken him somehow; but surely he could control it.

But the more he saw her, the more she captured him with every movement of her hands and hips, every nuance of her smile, the light in her soft eyes. The beauty no amount of makeup could create, no amount of surgery could buy. Just being Jennifer...

She landed in a heap of arms and legs at the other end of the slide, where she'd set up rubber bumpers to stop the kids getting hurt, and he laughed. She could make him happy with the simplest of acts, her uncomplicated, innate dignity…and she seized him heart and soul with her love for his children, and how she was healing them just by being herself.

Being Jennifer.

She untangled herself and jumped to her feet, yelling, "Let's all go together! A train!"

Noah lost his breath; a sharp lump lodged in his throat, blocking air. Her thin white summer shirt was wet, revealing every curve, each dusting freckle and the glow of her light-fawn skin. Her smile was radiant; she tossed her half-fallen plait off her breast to her back as if it were a nuisance.

Oh, to be that hand, that plait. To be able to touch her so casually…to touch her at all. Just to be free to touch her, to be a man again…

The gulp hurt him all the way down to his chest.

The kids beat her to the top of the slide, which she'd placed on a slow graded hill; they waited in line, Tim holding Cilla, Cilla holding Rowdy. Jennifer plumped down behind Tim, her hands at his waist, and she pushed off, with a loud cry, "Go!"

They didn't make it to the end, but nobody cared. Everyone was laughing too hard. Rowdy gave his cute, choking giggle, but Cilla and Tim were alive with the joy she brought them.

He couldn't stand it anymore. He'd been alone too long. He had to be a part of the fun.

"Let's make a bigger train!" he yelled, and ran for the hill. "I'll beat all of you!"

When he saw Cilla and Tim running to beat him—Cilla was *playing* with him—he choked up again. He deliberately tripped over nothing, just as Jennifer did when she knew they wanted to win, and landed splat on the wet, muddy grass face-first. "Ah, nuts!"

The kids cracked up when he lifted his face, showing it covered in dirt.

"Oh, get up, Brannigan. You're holding up the train!"

Noah grinned at Jennifer, standing over him like an impatient schoolmarm, if somewhat too wet and dirty for the job. An adorable paradox; the miracle he'd never hoped to find. He had to be careful, or he'd fall so hard and deep for her, he'd never climb out of it; but while he had this happiness, he'd grab at what he could.

He put his hand into her outstretched one, ready to help him up; but as he began getting up, she slipped away, letting him fall on his face again. "Ha! I got him, I got him!" she crowed to the kids, who were on the ground, pointing at him and cracking up again.

"Funny Daddy!" Rowdy cried.

"Silly Daddy," Cilla giggled.

"Silly Dad, he can't even get up by himself!" Tim shouted. He seemed to have no problem with Jennifer touching him— at least long enough to drop him on his face.

He looked up at the instigator of the scene, who winked at him, seeming totally unaware of what she'd just done for his family—or of her enticing state of semi-naked loveliness.

"I'll get you for that," he threatened, but his voice was a hoarse croak.

"Yeah, yeah, promises, Brannigan," she chanted, and ran for the slide. "Get in the line, kids. Big train time! I'm the driver this time!"

With a grin, Noah scrambled to his feet and joined onto Tim, who was at the back…and if Jennifer had deliberately avoided his touch by being the driver, it didn't matter. For this half hour, he had his family with him, his *happy* family, and it was a gift.

Another miracle at the March farm.

"Hey, Uncle Joe! We're here!" Rowdy cried, in his usual boisterous welcome. "We come for Timmy."

Jennifer's uncle came around the corner of the shop leading to the junkyard. "Hoy, little mate," Uncle Joe chuckled, sounding like a pirate. He'd never been on the sea apart from a few fishing expeditions, but Rowdy didn't know that. "And Miss Cilla—how's the prettiest girl this side of Brisbane?"

From behind Jennifer's skirt, Cilla smiled and waved. She wasn't quite sure of this big, bluff man, but if Tim and Rowdy liked him, she'd give him a chance.

"I called. I guess you were out the back." Jennifer smiled at her uncle. "Is he here?"

Joe nodded, his face tender. "He got here about an hour after school. He said he had permission. I gather he didn't," he sighed. "He's in a bad mood, Jenny—he doesn't even want me to help him. He just wants to bash nails into metal for a while. How about I bring him home in time for dinner?"

Jennifer sighed in turn. "Come for dinner—it might help."

Joe looked a bit shifty. "The Swans are playing tonight— St. Kilda. So how about he stays for dinner with me, watches the game, and then I bring him home? It's Friday—no harm in staying up a bit later, eh? It'll give him time to work it off, whatever it is."

After a brief hesitation, she nodded. "I'll check with Noah, and call you either way."

"It does him good being here, Jenny," Uncle Joe said quietly. "And it does me good, too. I like having the boy around. We have a project or two in the works…"

Jennifer touched his hand. "I know, Uncle Joe. A boy after your own heart, right?"

Joe chuckled, and cocked his head to where some strident banging was taking place out the back. "In some ways too old for his years—in others, just a boy. We're soul mates."

Working on her verandah an hour later, Noah saw Jennifer and the kids returning, laughing, and his heart lifted. She'd found Tim at Joe's again, he guessed.

Thank God for Jennifer—because of her and her uncle Joe, Tim had a permanent and safe place to run…and Cilla only disappeared next door.

But when they spilled out of the car and no Tim was in evidence, the familiar fear chilled his body, as if he'd been dropped in ice water. He snapped, "Where's Tim?"

Her face and voice casual—a mask for the tension Cilla didn't need—Jennifer said, "He and Uncle Joe have some special projects going on. He invited Tim for dinner and to watch the first Swans game of the season, if that's all right. He said he'd bring Tim home straight after—or before, if you prefer," she added quickly.

"Daddy, Jenny took me to the dolly museum today," Cilla blurted out, her eyes shining. "Her friend Brenda runs it. She's got more dollies than I ever saw!"

Noah felt the jerk inside him as he savagely reined in his anger over Joe's commandeering his son. Cilla was talking to him of her own free will… "A dolly museum? Wow—I didn't know there was one!" He waited for her answer, hoping she'd volunteer more information.

Cilla nodded vigorously, glowing with the joy of her outing. "Lots of grown-ups gave their dollies there, the lady said. There's really old dollies, and some talking dollies, and dressed-up dollies, and baby dollies that drink from bottles—"

"And soldier dollies, too, Daddy!" Rowdy added, so excited he was bouncing up and down.

Cilla pulled a face. "They got guns and big sticks, Daddy. Not *nice.*"

Noah laughed, and laid a hand on Cilla's curls. "Not nice for girls, but boys like them. Boys don't have good taste like girls. They like silly things like guns and sticks."

Cilla smiled up at him, and Noah almost gasped. He could barely remember when she'd smiled, just at him. "Did you like guns and sticks?" Her trusting expression said *of course you didn't*—and he smiled at her faith.

"Back in the Dark Ages of your youth," Jennifer murmured, laughter in her voice.

He shot her a mock-threatening look before returning to Cilla, telling her a truth that would disgust Rowdy if he was old enough to understand; but he was three, and Daddy could still do no wrong in his eyes. "I tried to like them, for a little while. I always liked LEGO and building blocks and drawing—but all my friends in the street wanted to play the rough stuff, so I had to pretend to like them, too."

Rowdy smiled at him in obvious pity. "Poor Daddy." He patted Noah's hand.

Cilla nodded thoughtfully in agreement with Rowdy, her brow wrinkled. "It must be hard to be a boy."

He choked on the laughter. So damn *adorable.* Cherishing the moment that was too rare—having a conversation with his daughter. "It is," he assured her, keeping a straight face and voice.

"You want to come see the dollies tomorrow, Daddy?"

Cilla wanted to spend time with him. Cilla invited him without being prompted!

*Hide the emotion. Don't scare her!* He nodded and smiled. "It's a date," he said solemnly.

In his peripheral vision he saw Jennifer swiping at her eyes. She knew.

"Jenny, I'm hungry," Rowdy said, with the angelic look he always used to get his way.

Jennifer laughed at that, and held out a hand to him. "Come on then, piggy, let's find something to eat. How about burgers tonight, and oven fries?"

"Yummy!" Rowdy cried, and scooted ahead of her around the side of the house. The screen door banged a moment later. Within moments, after a visible hesitation and a glance at her father, Cilla ran in after him.

Noah smiled after her, torn between joy at their first conversation in too long to remember, and wanting more in case it never happened again.

"Is it all right, Noah? About Tim, I mean? I told Uncle Joe I'd ask you and let him know."

He turned back to Jennifer, knowing he shouldn't indulge in the rare moment of being alone with her without Tim watching. "It's fine." His voice came out rough-edged. "If it makes Tim happy…"

"He's doing so much better." Jennifer half-reached out to him before she let her hand fall. "I know it's hard to see at times, but his teacher says he's settled down in class, and I can see him softening toward the kids here, as well. Before long, I think he'll be working on that cubby house with you."

*Not unless Belinda's found.* He couldn't blame her for not understanding. Tim might be healing with other people, but he'd only trust his father again if Belinda came back—and he no longer believed it was going to happen. Tim blamed him for his mother's disappearance, and barring a miracle, there was no way to change that.

He turned back to tearing off another plank. "That's great."

The tone of his voice made a lie of the words. *Just go away and leave me be...*

"I know you want more. You want him to be healed, to be able to accept what he can't change. You want him to stop resenting you for losing his mother and everything else that goes wrong in his life. But you're his father—who else can he blame? And no matter how he worries you, you've *got* him, Noah. He's here with you—he loves you dearly, even if you can't always see it. You don't know what a miracle that is."

Noah had looked up by the end of her first sentence, arrested by the taut, restrained passion in her voice. She stood before him, her right hand shaking, her eyes burning with a fire she was obviously about to share with him, whether he wanted it or not. "Are you okay?"

She dragged in a breath, two, before she spoke, yet it still came out choked with emotion, like a river rushing down-tide against a collapsing dam wall. "You lost Belinda, yet you still don't understand. There are thousands of people out there who wait years, and pay a fortune for what you have—a family. You have three beautiful, healthy children who adore you, despite their problems. I'd *die* for what you have!"

She pushed past him, running into the house with a stumbling step.

When the screen door slammed shut, Noah closed his eyes and dropped the ripped-up plank he still held. She was right, so right he was shocked, shamed by his wilful blindness all this time. His beautiful, healthy children were a gift he should never take for granted—and moving here, having Joe and Jennifer as a safe bolthole for the kids when they needed it, was a miracle he hadn't dared question, in case he woke up back in Sydney, still struggling to make it alone.

He was *blessed,* so much more so than he'd realised.

But it was *why* Jennifer had said it that shocked him the

most…all she'd half-said. All the painful hunger, the thwarted passion in her face and voice, which told him so much more than her stark words.

All this time he'd looked at her and wanted her, ached for her, been on-his-knees grateful for her, been amazed by her—but finally he was *seeing* her. Her words ripped away his blinders and showed her, not just as a woman, but as a person: a person whose empathy and strength came from a loss as profound and life-changing as his own.

All this time she'd listened to him, given to him—but she hadn't shared, and *he* hadn't listened. So damned scared he'd get too close to her, he'd missed all the signs.

No more. Right now, with the kids still awake, wasn't the time—but the first piece in the jigsaw of all she hadn't told him had just fallen into place, and judging by the anguish bursting from her just then, Jennifer needed to talk to someone about the tragedy in her past.

Desperately.

# CHAPTER SIX

HE WAS watching her, every time he thought she wasn't looking.

Talk about basket cases…!

Jennifer kept her attention on the kids as they ate, and again as she washed up; but it was hard to avoid him when he insisted on helping bath Cilla and Rowdy and putting them to bed. Then he also wiped the dishes before he returned to work.

It was even harder to act normal when he kept *looking* at her as if he was waiting for her to burst out again.

*Well, you did before…*

*I am a strong woman. I do not need to lean on a man. I do not need a family to complete me. I can stand alone. I have a good life!*

Her hand might be shaking, but it was a fine tremor hardly noticeable, she thought. She had it under control this time. So what if a few plates fell back into the dishwater? Soap made them slippery. He couldn't make anything out of that, surely.

He was still watching.

Would he never *speak?* She kept waiting for him to go off, like a bomb with a faulty timer. She refused to say a word beyond anything to do with the kids. He was nothing but her neighbour. They had an arrangement to eat together while he worked on her house. An attraction was there, but they'd submerged it. They'd agreed on that—so why did it feel so wrong?

*Because you're lying to yourself.* It was a truth she couldn't deny. Even now, she had to fight the shiver of pleasure when his arms brushed hers just to pick up a plate to dry. *If this is attraction submerged, how bad would it become if it came out into the open?*

"You need a haircut," she blurted, and almost gasped. Where had that come from? "It—it's a bit shaggy," she added, feeling defensive with the look of hidden amusement he aimed at her.

He shrugged. "I've been meaning to get it cut for a while, but life's busy." He ran a hand through the length of it—and she gulped, following every movement of his fingers through the long, silky mass.

"I can cut it for you, if you like." Good grief. What was wrong with her tonight? But she held her ground when he lifted a brow in inquiry. "I did a year of hairdressing, you know, when I was sixteen. Before I decided it wasn't for me, and went back to school."

"So if it wasn't for you, why should I trust you with my hair?"

He was laughing at her, and it made her smile. "I learned enough to do a wash and simple cut." To her horror, she was almost whispering. What must he think of her? She rushed into speech. "I won't nick your ears or cut your neck…or cut it too short. It's too beautiful to give it a buzz cut…"

Oh, help, she'd done it again. Staring at him like a loon, now offering to cut his hair—calling it beautiful. What an infatuated fool he must think she was!

"Don't worry. It—it was a stupid idea." She stared down at her feet, wishing a black hole would miraculously open up and transport her to a parallel universe. "You have work to do…"

"Actually I'd appreciate a cut if you have time for it?"

His voice was soft, knowing. He'd seen her embarrassment, and was helping her out. Again. Would she never stop making an idiot of herself over him?

Yet, though she knew she should reject his offer and keep what shards of her pride remained intact, she pulled out a chair for him. "Sit." She got the kit she rarely used, but hadn't thrown out. "I can't believe I still have this kit. My friends Veronica and Jessie call me a squirrel, the way I won't throw out anything useful."

He laughed. "We all have our faults." He tipped his head forward while she laid the plastic cloak over his shoulders. "You're not going to wash my hair for me first? I hear it makes it easier to give an accurate cut…"

His tone was pure mischief: the same tone he'd used when he offered to put his shirt back on. She put the Velcro pieces together. "I have a bottle of water," she informed him primly, and began squirting around his head before combing it through.

It was intimate—too intimate. Running her fingers through his hair, touching his scalp—she might as well have washed his hair. Noah made a tiny, masculine sound as he leaned back into the touch. "Mmm, that's good."

"I'm supposed to massage it a bit before I cut, to stimulate your scalp," she said, then closed her eyes. *You idiot, why not just tell him you can't keep your hands off him?*

"It's stimulating all right," he said softly.

Jennifer almost gasped. The meaning was too strong to miss.

"I'm going to cut now. Lean back a bit more."

This was such a personal thing. It had never felt this intense with customers—even with Mark. Threading her fingers through Noah's hair before cutting it felt so sensuous; she felt stark, her desire totally open to him.

Trying to avoid nervous babble, she remained silent, except to say "left" or "right," "up" or "down." Hand through again…lift hair…cut. Yes. That's it. Cut. Don't just touch and let it fall…

Her throat began to ache with the constant rushing of her breath. Surely he could hear the way she gulped down air with each touch—a touch that became more of a caress each time?

She couldn't help it…how did she stop? Body and heart were betraying her will. A strong woman? Ha! She was a quivering mass of jelly…aching for him to turn around, look at her, slow and wanting…take her in his arms, and—

"I think you're done," she announced eventually, despising herself for the breathless way she said it. Foolish woman!

He looked in the mirror at every angle, and nodded. "A great job. Thanks, Jennifer."

He wasn't smiling, either…and the *look* in his eyes, dark and lush—

"It's almost dark," she said when she couldn't stand the silence, his closeness, anymore. "Soon you won't be able to work."

"I brought spotlights," he said, his voice rough with all they weren't saying. "I want to keep working until Joe brings Tim back."

"Then off you go. I can sweep up the mess." Turning her face from his, before the temptation clawing at her came bursting to life, she pulled off the protective cloak.

"If you need anything, call me."

"What do you imagine I'll need?" she asked before she could stop herself.

She felt rather than saw his shrug. "Maybe to talk to someone? It's obvious you need to talk to somebody, Jennifer." He stood up.

She spun around to face him. "Why? Because I happened

to mention that you've got so many wonderful blessings in your life you're taking for granted?"

"I think it was what you didn't say that needs to come out," he said quietly, his gaze steady on her face: warm and caring, deep with unspoken male empathy in those deep maple syrup eyes. It made her shiver in longing. Strong, beautiful, raw masculinity just a breath away...

And the urge to tell him everything was growing stronger, more unbearable, every time he was near her. The urge to haul him against her, and—

"You think I'm so weak I need to speak to a near-stranger about my personal concerns?" she snapped, to hide it.

"I think you're the strongest woman I've ever known and we've never been strangers. Some people know each other from the start and you can be around others all your life and never get close." His voice was rough-edged, deep and hot, and she ached and burned. Just one step, one touch, and she'd be in his arms. "I also think you're falling down, Jennifer, and too strong and proud to admit you need anyone."

She jerked back in reaction to his insight.

"Even the strongest people fall down sometimes," he went on, ignoring her upflung hand, trying to put distance between them: a pitiful barrier. "We all need someone to give back now and then. I've been there, and I refused help, Jennifer—and you know the consequences. If I'd reached out and admitted my family needed help before Belinda disappeared, when she was ill with depression and I knew she wasn't coping, my kids might still have their mother."

Jennifer repressed the shudder. What he said was true; but though it might hurt Noah like crazy to have this life, she felt sick at the thought of knowing him only as another woman's husband...

*He is another woman's husband, until Belinda is found.*

She started when he touched her cheek with a finger. "You've given my family so much. I'm not asking for anything more—just let me be here for you when you need someone, Jennifer. I'll catch you. I won't let you fall."

*Oh God, he was touching her.*

The power of it left her breathing hard and shallow, her body weak and trembling, filling her with hope for what she couldn't have; she knew that. But the tenderness in his face, in his voice, undid her; temptation clawed and bit at her with relentless aching. If he had any idea what allowing him in would cost her…

She couldn't turn away, could only look up at him, half-mesmerised; but still her rebel mouth spoke a truth she'd give anything if it weren't so. "If I'm going to fall, let me fall. You can't save me, Noah. You don't have the right."

His hand dropped from her face.

After a few minutes of a silence that screamed his protest, he said, his voice neutral, "Thanks for dinner and the haircut, Jennifer."

She shrugged, and found her voice. "Just hamburgers and chips, and ten minutes to cut your hair. It's no big deal."

"It means a lot to me, to the kids…they love you, Jennifer. And you don't know what it means to me to see them smiling and—and happy again."

Her mouth flattened. The choked tone, filled with emotion, left her longing to reach out, to touch him. *You can't!* "It's a business arrangement." Refusing to admit the truth—that the Brannigans had become her lifeline to brittle sanity.

There was too much to lose in getting close to him—for them all.

She jumped when his hand touched her shoulder. "I know I have no right to ask for more, and I don't—but at least let me be your friend, Jennifer."

Treacherous currents of warm need flooded a heart and soul empty for too long. She squeezed her eyes shut, allowing one moment, two, of not being alone.

Of being with Noah, who must never mean this much to her. Beautiful, forbidden sweetness and desire…

She stepped out from under his hand, feeling it like a physical wrench, the loss and the longing. "Don't you understand? I can *never* be your friend."

She strode into her bedroom, shut the door and pulled the curtains tight, before he said another word and totally shattered her fragile illusion that she had a life, that she was happy, that life was good.

This had gone too far, and they'd barely touched. She had to sell up and leave this place before—before she started *thinking*…

Dry-eyed and her mind burning-hot, she stared through the curtains onto the night, knowing that he was out there, working. Just because he was there, she was a quivering mess of aching femininity and hope. She'd been doing nothing but *thinking* about it from the moment she'd seen his face.

*Lovers.* If she stayed here another week without making the change, it would happen—she knew it. He had to know, too. The look in his eyes, the tension in his body when he was near her, told her she wasn't alone in this. One touch, and the uncontrolled flight, body, heart and soul came. This was a once-in-a-lifetime, never-again occurrence. She'd loved Mark dearly for many years, and enjoyed his touch; but she'd barely touched Noah's hand, and she was so *alive,* so tuned to him she could think of nothing else when he was near her.

One more touch, and they'd become lovers…

Beautiful, too brief, and soon over. There could be no promises with a man who wasn't officially separated from his missing wife, not divorced and not quite a widower…and Noah still didn't know why she'd never marry again.

She closed her eyes, his words already haunting her. *You're falling down, Jennifer.*

But for the first time, she wasn't grieving for Cody, or her broken marriage.

*Noah. Tim, Cilla, Rowdy.* Right now, when she admitted to herself she'd give up her hope of life itself just to have the right to be with them a little longer; that she'd give up anything to just touch Noah—she knew she would lose them before long.

And the pain of it was just the same as she'd faced two years ago.

She was absolutely crazy about all four of the Brannigans. They'd taken her heart and soul—and they belonged to another woman: a woman more *here,* more *alive* in her absence than she'd be if she were here.

Joe dropped a sleepy, grinning Tim home after ten that night.

Smiling, no doubt, because he'd had fun with Joe—and because Noah was working hard on the verandah and Jennifer was nowhere to be seen.

"Hey, Dad." Tim waved at him, his eyes heavy. "I'm going in to Jen."

"Did you have fun, mate?" Noah called as his son half-stumbled toward the front door.

"The Swans won, Dad! It was a cracker of a game to start the Season—a pearler!"

Noah smothered a grin, and lifted a brow in Joe's direction. "That's great, mate!"

Tim waved again, and went inside, calling to Jennifer.

Joe came over to where he worked: a casual stroll that didn't fool him for a moment. "They all treat Jenny as if she's their mother now, don't they?" he asked quietly.

He didn't answer at first; he'd been expecting this for the

past week or more. Nodding, he said, just as softly, "They're still so little. They need a mother."

"And you need a child-carer, dinner-maker and the like. Your moving here provided the ideal situation for you all, you might say." Joe's voice was dry.

"Just say it, Joe," Noah said wearily. "I've had a long day. I'm too tired to talk in code."

"Has Jenny told you about herself at all? About her past, and why she came here?"

The blunt question, also, wasn't unexpected. "Only that she's divorced and her ex was obviously into nasty labels about her."

Joe sighed and rubbed his forehead, obviously searching for words.

"Don't break her confidence, Joe," he said quietly, and tore up another plank. Almost the last, and he could start re-building. "She wouldn't appreciate you saying anything to me. She'll tell me if and when she wants to." He hoped.

"That's the trouble," Joe snapped. "That's what you don't understand, Noah. Jenny *never* tells anyone anything about her private business. She never even talked to her parents after it all happened, or during. She went to some grief class things, but never told us, her own family. If she tells you—" he thumped a fist against his open palm "—if she does, it's because…" He swore: a long string of words that showed his frustration. "If she tells you, it's because you mean more to her than anyone else in her life. And you might want that…or you might just want to help her. And it might help, for a little while. But when you don't find whatever it is you came here for, and move on—and we both know you will," he added dryly, "when you go, and take those kids from her, she'll break."

Break.

Not *break down,* not *break her heart.* Just—*break.* Not a warning, not a threat; just a statement of fact.

Jennifer would break—and he would be the one to break her.

He didn't know what to do or say to that. How did he say he'd already pushed Jennifer onto that path, because he couldn't handle all her giving, and not giving anything back but a stupid verandah, so she could sell up and leave him?

*Leave me?*

Was he taking the family life she'd given back to him for granted, even knowing it could only be temporary? When it was over, would he resent her for having her own life and choices, when Belinda had left him with none, trapped and re-senting everything and everyone who *did* have a choice in life?

Joe nodded. "It's there, isn't it? You're not just taking all she's got to give you and the kids. You want more. You want something with my Jenny, at least for now—but until you're free to reach out and take it, until you know what happened to your wife and you've worked out things with young Tim, stop messing with my girl's emotions. You've been to hell and back—but so has she." He sighed. "The attraction between you is so strong even an old fool like me can feel it. She's dreaming, Noah…and she loves those kids of yours so much. Like a mother."

The unwanted insight broadsided him. Joe was right; and Jennifer was right, too—they could never be friends. The wanting was agony already, and it was growing every day. He could easily imagine himself old and grey and still in pain with wanting Jennifer—but not just in bed. Every small thing he did with her, every smile or flick back of her plait, every time she hugged his kids or looked at him with that half-hidden yearning, he soared with the joy of it: of family, of be-longing—of being a man desired by a woman with so much inner beauty she made him ache.

And if he took the chance, his family would fall apart.

One or the other. Jennifer or his son; both fragile, both part of his life and, yes, damn it, his heart. He cared about Jennifer. So who did he break?

He wanted to hit something, because he knew it wasn't a contest.

As much as he loved Tim, the resentment had grown from a tiny kernel to a massive forest inside Noah's heart during the past couple of weeks. For how many years would Tim's happiness depend on his father struggling alone? Did he have to give up what remained of his youth for Tim's security? Leaving Jennifer behind would lead to a lifetime of regret…

*You'll break her.*

"Uncle Joe, did you want a coffee or a beer before you head home?"

Noah looked up at the frost in her tone, hidden well beneath a veneer of polite welcome—but it was there. As her glance flicked to him, he saw the speculation…the accusation.

She'd heard—perhaps not all of it, but she'd heard—heard what Uncle Joe said about what he, Noah, might mean to her. If he'd had any chance of giving back to her, of hearing the story that might take some of the burden from her giving shoulders, he'd just lost it.

No way. *No!* He wouldn't let her withdraw—he needed her too much.

Yet, wasn't that the problem? He needed her—but what did Jennifer need?

*She's been to hell and back…*and he was adding to her pain.

None of this was Jennifer's fault. Nothing could change for them while he was still technically married…and while he allowed Tim's fears and terrors to rule the family's life. While he allowed Belinda's ghost to haunt them all, even people who'd never known her.

There was only one option: closure. He had to find it.

## CHAPTER SEVEN

HE HAD to do this. *It's for Tim and Cilla.*

Noah stood outside the door in the children's ward at a private hospital near Lismore, an hour north of Hinchliff, reading the sign in silent loathing. *Maggie Horner, Social Worker And Grief Counsellor.*

He'd thought he'd seen the last of the professionals trained to help him—making him feel like not only a basket case, but a bad husband and a failure of a father. *It's not your fault, Noah, you're only human. You can't take responsibility for everything that goes wrong in the lives of those you love.*

It was just a pretty way of calling him a control freak. How could they know anything? They learned it all from books, got a degree, and thought they knew life.

When had their wife taken off and left them with three kids under six?

*This isn't for me. I have to learn how to help Tim and Cilla. I can't keep leaving it to Jennifer. I can't make the kids—or Jennifer—dependent. It isn't fair.*

He pushed open the door—and rocked back on his feet in shock when he saw one of only two occupants of the room.

Jennifer gasped and stared at him in turn.

"Well, here we are," a brisk woman in dark blue pants and a

striped uniform shirt said cheerfully. "Welcome, Mr. Brannigan. I'm Rachel Howe, Ms Horner's receptionist. Ms Horner sends her apologies. There was an emergency in the E.R."

"I hope everything's all right," Jennifer said, her voice stifled, at the same time Noah wondered what kind of emergency could possibly require a social worker.

"A baby drowned," the receptionist said, her voice dropping to real sorrow. "It will hit the local papers tomorrow. Maggie will stay with the parents for the next few hours, helping the family through as much as they'll let her."

Jennifer gasped again, her eyes full of tears. A shaking hand lifted to her mouth.

"I'm sorry, Mrs. March," Rachel rushed to say. "I shouldn't have said anything, after your son's death—"

Jennifer paled so quickly, Noah thought she might faint.

"I'm so sorry, Mrs. March," Rachel went on, looking uncertain and guilty. "I didn't mean to break confidentiality—"

Jennifer looked at her, but seemed to see right through her. She looked as clear and delicate as blown glass, and just as easily shattered. "It's all right. It's not a state secret."

"Maggie tried to call you both, but you'd left," the receptionist rushed on. "She left messages on your phones, but I guess you'd turned them off while you were driving. Maggie noticed you two are neighbours, so she thought you might take advantage of the two hours' crèche arrangement for Mr. Brannigan's children, and maybe go for coffee? There's a lovely café just down the road that serves a good lunch under umbrellas in the sun…"

"Thank you," Noah said gravely. "Jennifer?"

The question wasn't a ploy. The words she'd spoken the other night burned in his brain like a bushfire that wouldn't go out. *I'll never be your friend.*

Too much between them, and never enough.

After a long hesitation, she nodded without looking at him. "Thank you for letting us know," she said to the receptionist, still sounding stifled.

Noah's mind was spinning as he opened the door for her. Ever since her outburst last week and Joe's warning, he hadn't tried to get her to open up. He thought he'd known her problem—but now he knew Jennifer could have children. She'd had a son—and he'd died.

*I'd die for what you have!*

The pieces finally fit.

"Would you like coffee, or lunch? It's almost eleven-thirty," he said, for the sake of something to say.

They stepped out into the bright autumn sunshine. A clear, windless day, warm enough but without the intense dry pulsing of the recent heatwave. The street stretched out, long and straight, with waving banners on the streetlamps, announcing an upcoming festival.

Jennifer didn't appear to notice. "I think I'd throw up if I ate now," she mumbled. "The poor, poor parents. Poor baby, so short a life…"

Filled with compassion like a wave hitting him from behind, he put an arm around her shoulders. "Makes me thank God for my kids," he said, in a low voice.

She didn't shake him off, as he'd half expected; nor did she turn her face to him, but remained looking straight ahead. "That's why you came, isn't it? To learn how to best help Tim and Cilla?" The question sounded blind, as if she wandered in a dark maze, and familiarity was comfort. Asking him about his life as usual, taking nothing in return.

Being Jennifer.

"You know my story, Jennifer. You know why I'm here." He pulled her back as she was about to walk straight into a massive crack in the sidewalk. "I haven't kept any secrets."

*Liar.* But now wasn't the time to tell her that.

Finally she turned to him. Her eyes were fierce. "Just say it, Noah."

A furious opening, but if it was all he'd get, he'd take it. As he steered her into an open courtyard with tables and umbrellas, he asked, "How old was your son?"

"Three." The word was curt.

He shut his eyes for a moment. He understood so much now. No wonder she'd had that look on her face when she'd first seen Rowdy. "What was his name?"

Something passed over her face; her eyes were cold and dead. "Cody James McBride."

"Cody. That's a nice name." *How lame was that, Brannigan?*

Her smile was no more than a slight curl of the ends of her mouth. "Mark picked it, but I liked it, too."

After a long hesitation, she answered what he didn't know how to ask. "He had Cystic Fibrosis. He choked to death—it was like drowning. His lungs just couldn't keep stretching."

She spoke as if it was something she'd rehearsed for a play, just reading it aloud; and he wondered how many times she'd had to say it, just like that, to get the tone down pat. The tone said, *keep your distance. You know what happened, now back off.*

Joe had been right. Jennifer was not one who wanted her wounds touched.

"How long have you been going to the counselling sessions?" he asked gently, taking her hand in his.

She let it lie there resistless. Her eyes were like pools drained of water…empty. "I began in the hospital in Newcastle, when I first found out about Cody's illness."

*I began.* Not *we.* That told him far more about Mark McBride than he'd wanted to know—he'd left Jennifer alone with the grief and guilt.

*Yeah, you know nothing about male denial and running away, do you?* his mind mocked him. *That's why, three years after Belinda ran, you're finally reaching out—but only for the kids' sake; you don't need help from outsiders.*

*You'll take it from Jennifer, though,* his mind mocked him again.

"And you kept it up when you moved here?" He heard the strange, choked sound of his voice, and wondered if she'd pick up on it.

She shrugged. "A few sessions here and there, when I need to. I've become good friends with Veronica and Jessie from the group. We meet every second Saturday for lunch—we all like to quilt as well, and started a quilting circle." She smiled, but it was remote, untouched by sweetness or sorrow. "They have kids now, and I have my business, so Saturdays or the occasional Wednesday evening works for us all."

He frowned. "But you haven't gone out on a Wednesday since…"

*Since I've been taking it for granted she has nothing to do but mind my kids for me, or have my family to stay for dinner.*

Selfish jerk! He hadn't thought of Jennifer at all—maybe as a desirable woman, but as a *person* with needs? He'd thought he'd written the book on loss and suffering—but what he'd written was a treatise on selfish need: a blindness to anything but his needs, and that of the kids.

The waitress came then, and took their orders. Once she'd gone, he lifted their hands upward, so their fingers laced through each other's. "Damn, I'm sorry, Jennifer," he said quietly. "You've been putting your life on hold for me, for the kids."

Her eyes weren't empty now, but gentle, eager and shy. "Don't apologise, Noah. It's been nice to be part of family life again." Her gaze landed on their linked hands, and she bit her lip and pulled away. "For a little while, anyway."

"Why won't you marry again?" He could have hit himself for the bluntness of the question, but it had been burning in him since before they'd met. He *had* to know.

A hand scrubbed her forehead, tugged at a lock of loose hair waving in a light breeze just springing up, pushing the hair behind her ear. Then she began twisting her plait around a finger. "You want it all, don't you?" She sounded so tired: a weary Madonna. "After Cody was born, they tested us to see who the carrier was, and why Cody had CF so badly. It seems I'm a freak medical case—the doctors haven't come across it before. There is CF in my family—but my genome is so dominant they believe any child I have would be almost certain to be born with the disease…and I won't play Russian roulette with a baby's life, just to fulfil my desires."

Noah knew he'd never seen anything sadder than this quiet, giving woman, a woman more born to be a mother than any he'd ever known, accepting that she'd always be alone.

It was only when his arms and body were warm and her head was resting on his shoulder that he knew he'd gone to her. "I'm sorry, Jennifer," he whispered, holding her so close she was a part of him; the ache threatening to burst in him.

"It's all right," she whispered, pulling back to smile up at him.

"Couldn't you do IVF? The kind where there's a donor mother?" he blurted.

She smiled again, but with more sadness than any woman as giving as Jennifer should have to know. "I could. My sisters have all offered to be the egg donor. But that isn't the point." She sighed. "As selfish as it sounds, I want *my* baby, not someone else's—and I don't want to be a—"

"Single parent?" he filled in, when she bit her lip. "It's okay, Jennifer. Raising kids alone isn't something I'd recommend to everyone."

"You don't know how lucky you are," she mumbled, low.

Noah flinched. He'd done it again. "Jennifer…"

"Don't." She shrugged. "This isn't a Greek tragedy, you know. I have a good life. I have a wonderful family, friends who care about me, a life that's mostly full and busy. It's not the life I planned for myself, but it's still good."

"You could still marry a man with kids, who doesn't want any more." He stumbled over the words. Damn, it sounded too close to a proposal.

She didn't even seem to notice; she was already shaking her head. "I could never marry a man for his kids alone—I'd have to marry for love." She gave him a watery smile. "And while I'm sure I'd love his kids, it wouldn't be right or fair to them, if I couldn't love them as much as I loved Cody. All I ever wanted was to get married and have four or five kids— but if they weren't mine…" she trailed off, shrugging; but it was eloquent enough.

He frowned again. "You don't think you could mother kids if they weren't your own?" It sounded crazy to him. She gave love to the kids she minded so naturally, so lavishly. It seemed impossible that she could have given more to her own son.

"Not the way a child deserves to be loved." She pulled away, discreetly mopping her face with the serviette. "Here comes the waitress. Just as well I don't bother much with makeup, or I'd look like that sad-faced clown painting right now." She smiled again. "I promise you, I don't cry on people often."

As the waitress put down the coffee and cake and bustled off again, he looked down at Jennifer. So *close,* those wet cheeks, the salty, pretty mouth. He'd never wanted to kiss her more, and that was a big statement, given the hot, sleepless nights he'd endured, dreaming of her face, her touch.

But she moved away, sitting up straight, and smiling again. She'd closed the subject of her past, the life she'd chosen. She'd said enough; she didn't feel sorry for herself, wasn't angry or in the throes of unresolved grief. She had a life, and was moving on.

Then why did it feel so wrong?

"You shouldn't be alone," he muttered, as savage as he felt at the thought of her growing old, still minding other people's kids, spending day after day with reminders of what she could never have. "You were born to be a mother." *And some kids need a mother as good as you.*

She looked away. "The world isn't perfect. Babies all over the world were born to live, not die. People weren't born to starve or live in war zones. We don't all get our dreams, Noah."

Who was she trying to fool, herself or him? "I suppose you sing 'Always Look on the Bright Side of Life' whenever you feel sorry for yourself," he shot back, furious. Why, he didn't know—but he couldn't stand this quiet acceptance. She should be yelling and screaming at the unfair hand life had dealt her, fighting somehow.

She turned back then, with a lifted brow. "Would you dish out a Pollyanna crack if I said yes?" Her grin was both mischievous and challenging.

Without warning, warm laughter bubbled up and burst out of him. "Probably," he said when he finally got control of himself again.

"Then I refuse to answer on the grounds that it might incriminate me."

He chuckled again, and tapped her chin. "You're an amazing woman, you know that?" How she'd gotten him from grief to fury to amusement so fast was beyond him; but Jennifer could make him *feel* more, and feel it faster, than anyone he'd ever known.

She lifted her coffee cup, and toasted him with a grin. "Even we incorrigibly cheerful types have our surprises."

Obviously, he thought as he crammed some cake in his

mouth. She'd done nothing but surprise him from the moment
he'd seen her. How her ex had been stupid enough to lose her
once he had her, Noah couldn't begin to understand.

*Don't go there.* It was dangerous enough that his dreams
were filled with her; daydreams were strictly off-limits. If
things were different…but he was still a nowhere man—and
though he'd been trying like crazy to change that, some things
were beyond his control.

His vow was still intact, set in stone by the suffering of an
innocent child. He couldn't have Jennifer—and that, too, was
end of subject.

"No, don't come and get him just yet," Uncle Joe said with a
mysterious air the next day when Jennifer called. "Tim and I
are *very* busy right now. Give us until six?"

Jennifer sighed and looked out the window. There was no
sign of Noah as yet, but he'd stressed he wanted Tim here
when he got home from a quote on a new industrial complex
in Brisbane city. Tim had spent every afternoon at Joe's for
the past week, taking his new best friend Ethan with him. Tim
had an air of hidden excitement the past few days, growing
so big by last night he'd only picked at his vegetables.

It was almost time to reveal the secret, whatever it was—
so what did she do? Alienate the parent or force the child
home, and ruin his big surprise?

*Come on, Pollyanna, fix the situation for everyone as always.*

She had to take the fall, one way or the other.

Since their talk in Lismore, Noah had been acting strangely
with her. She couldn't put her finger on what the difference
was—maybe he didn't know it, but it was in the way he
looked at her, both with him and with the kids. Something had
changed between them that day, and they couldn't go back
now, but there was a feeling of—waiting…

As if he was going to just pack up and disappear one day, and never come back.

"Sure," she said to Joe, knowing she took a risk in not following a parent's dictum; she could lose her licence for it. But she wasn't paid to mind Tim; she'd refused all payment for him being here in the afternoons, so this wasn't a professional, but personal matter.

And she knew Noah would never make an official complaint, in any case.

She just hoped he came home after six—

But Murphy's Law seemed to apply to everything that happened between them; and of course he drove in at five-thirty. "Hey, kids, I'm home—and I have presents for everyone!" he yelled from the car.

"Presents!" Cilla and Rowdy squealed in sync, and jumped up from their painting game and rushed out the back door.

With a sense of fatality she'd felt since saying "sure" to Joe, she followed the kids. She should have known Noah would have a good reason for demanding Tim's return. Now she'd not only disregarded a parent's rule, she'd ruined his joy in present time for his children.

The set smile was already on his face when she came around the side of the house to the pressed-dirt driveway. "I hear Tim's still at Uncle Joe's," he said over the kids' excited chatter: Cilla over her talking, feeding dolly; Rowdy over the big, shiny black water gun that squirted water balls.

She had no right to argue the rightness of her decision at this moment. "I'm sorry, Noah. Uncle Joe said he's almost finished his big project…"

"And you couldn't say no." Noah's shrug was weary; all the happiness evident in his voice moments before was gone.

"I had no right," she said bluntly, unable to stop the half-defensive self-condemnation. "I know that."

"You care for him more often than I do, so let's not go there." The tiredness in him seemed endemic, reaching out to touch her, feeling worse for its not being physical.

"No, you're the guilt specialist. Nobody has as much right to feel bad about themselves as you do." The words popped out before she knew she'd spoken; she stared at him in horror.

He'd stiffened by the end of the first sentence. "I wasn't aware it was a right." He began ushering the kids into his truck. "I think of it more as a life sentence—but by all means, Jennifer, indulge as much as you want, if you like it." He strapped Cilla into her seat.

*That's right, Jennifer, let the man come home with gifts for his kids and destroy it for him...*she groaned to herself. What was *wrong* with her? How many more times would she need to apologise to him before she began getting things right? "I have dinner ready," she said quietly.

He strapped Rowdy in next. He was happily playing with his squirt gun, pretending to hit Cilla over and over. She didn't notice, too busy feeding her dolly. "I think we've imposed enough on you for one day. You haven't had time to yourself in weeks as it is. It's Wednesday—you should call your quilting friends and have some fun. We'll go get Tim."

Peace and quiet...just minutes ago she'd registered how tired she was; now she had the prospect of a night to herself, all she saw was hours of silence, no childish chatter, no hugs, no *family*. Just spending a night alone.

There was nothing to say. She'd infringed on his rights with his children too much lately. It wasn't as if—as if she was anything to them. "Good idea, I will call them."

She made herself smile and wave to the kids as Noah pulled out his phone and called Uncle Joe. "Joe, I'm on my way over to get some dinner, so I'll get Tim...yes, I know, thanks anyway, but I need to get some dinner anyway—what?" The easy tone turned hard. "What do you mean he's not there? Where did he go—?" He listened for a minute, his nostrils flared and his eyes dark. "It's a surprise. I see. How long has he been gone…an *hour?* What happened to him? Was he upset? Did he say anything? Do you know where my son is, Joe? *Do you know where Tim is?*"

The panic in his voice would have been out of place for most parents, but not for Noah—never for Noah.

Feeling sick with fear and wretched guilt, Jennifer was already strapped into the front passenger seat by the time Noah flung himself in the truck.

# CHAPTER EIGHT

"I CAN'T tell you—I promised the lad I'd keep his secret," Joe was saying for the fourth time. "I'm sure he's not in any danger. I swear he hasn't run off, Noah."

"Promises. Swearing. What is that supposed to mean?" Noah snapped. "You think it counts for *anything* with me, when it's just about dark and my son's missing?" Noah's voice cracked; he pulled out his phone again.

"Don't do it!" Again Joe reached out to stop him. "The little lad was that excited, Noah. If you call Sherbrooke on him now, you'll ruin it all."

"So you keep saying. Tell me why!" When Joe shook his head, Noah lost it. "Then damn your promises and Tim's surprise! My eight-year-old son is *missing,* it's almost night and you expect me to—"

"To trust your son! Yes, I do!" Joe snapped back. "Give him ten more minutes! That's all I'm asking."

"That's what I did with Belinda," he snarled at the older man. "I trusted her to come home! After my five-year-old son called me to come home because the babysitter had to go and Rowdy was screaming and he couldn't get him out of the cot, I came home to find my wife gone—not her things, just her. I gave her ten more minutes, and another ten, and another, hoping she was just shopping, visiting someone I didn't know—anything but the truth. And then when she was put on the missing persons list, all I could think was, *what if I hadn't given her ten minutes?* What if, in those ten minutes I hesitated, she was abducted, raped or murdered, and I could have saved her? If there's one thing experience has taught me, it's that it's better to have my son alive and mad at me. If I can save my son's life by being *safe rather than sorry,* I'll do it even if he hates me!"

Joe's resistance tumbled down like a house of cards out in the wind; his hand dropped from the phone. Noah flipped it open, finger poised to hit speed dial 1—Police Sergeant Fred Sherbrooke's home number.

"Noah."

The touch of Jennifer's hand on his didn't feel as Joe's had—trying to stop him; it trembled slightly. "Noah, I understand—I want him found as much as you do, and it's my fault this happened. But before we call Fred, why not call his friends' houses? He's just a kid, Noah, and he's been so happy, so settled lately. If he's just playing, and lost track of time…"

The good sense beneath the guilt in her words stopped him, just as he was about to ignore her and hit the green call button. He heard all she wasn't saying: *he's only little, he wouldn't notice the dark coming if he's having fun with a friend.*

"I already called Ethan's house on the way, but I can call Miss Greenwood and get the numbers of Tim's other friends…"

He heard what she was saying. Tim was making friends here; a sign of healing, even if he wasn't ready to admit to that. Here in Hinchliff, the kids either didn't know or didn't care about the family's history. Tim was just a normal kid, one of twenty kids of a single parent.

And he'd thanked God for it.

If he blew it now by overreacting…the story would be

around town in hours, and they'd rehash all they knew about Belinda's disappearance, and their theories on why she'd run. Just like in Sydney—a repetition of the reason Tim had begun running away in the first place. *I'm going to find Mummy, then they'll all stop being nasty!*

Everything else Jennifer hadn't said came whispering into his brain. Tim hadn't run away now for almost two months; the change of scene, school and friends, and Jennifer's healing presence, had worked the miracle he'd prayed for when he'd left Sydney and all its memory. One misstep now and he could undo all the progress Tim had made.

But the one thing Jennifer could never understand was the ghost stalking him night and day, the spectre of history repeating—the history that had almost repeated so many times, every time Cilla or Tim disappeared. *Oh God, if his precious boy was truly missing, in danger...*

"I *can't*," he rasped. Feeling the line in the sand shifting with the wind, as it had done almost every day throughout the past three years, he pressed the button, spoke to Fred briefly and then stood there, feeling guilty and lost and angry.

He started when a pair of gentle arms slid around his waist. "I understand. It's all right," she whispered from behind him. She held him close, giving him her caring and strength at the moment he'd never felt so alone with his fears.

Without conscious thought or decision he turned his face. "Thank you," he whispered back, in a tight, halting rasp. Two words hadn't taken so long to say since the time he'd heard four fateful words: *your wife is missing.*

Tonight wasn't about Belinda; she'd been fading from his thoughts for a long time, but now she wasn't here with him at all. Usually she seemed to hover over him like some damned ghost ship packed with sackloads of guilt and regret. But at this moment he was just a worried dad, with a beautiful, gentle woman who loved his son and made him feel like a *man* again. A woman who was looking at him with so much longing in her eyes it turned his fears inside-out; with so much *faith,* he began to believe.

"Tim will come home to us," she mouthed without sound. She was with him…and for the first time in years, he didn't feel so damned alone.

Without conscious thought or decision, he moved across the inch that had been separating them for too long, and brushed his mouth over hers.

Could a first kiss be any more wrong? Wrong time, wrong place, wrong everything. He wasn't free; his son was missing; his other kids were four feet away, playing with their new toys—and Joe, who'd warned him against taking things further with Jennifer, was watching grimly. Noah could feel the anger simmering in him.

But it was all vague, peripheral, technical; it didn't matter. What was real was that Jennifer's breath hitched; he felt her breasts flatten against his shoulder and arm. Her eyes filled with a yearning and arousal so strong, his entire body tightened in reaction.

The current of wanting snapped together. Finally, contact…

One moment in time, that was all; then she pulled back, her face carefully controlled. "Tim!" she called, waving to the left. Noah, lost still in the feeling of being a man, not just a dad, took a few seconds longer to react.

And then it was too late.

The beaming boy proudly riding a slightly lopsided bike— this must have been his project with Joe—vanished in an instant, and the resentful rebel in a child's body replaced him. The slitted eyes, the mouth turned down. The suspicious boy, the guard dog in human form had returned by necessity.

*Tim had seen him kissing Jennifer.*

"Hey, mate!" he called, going into automatic damage control. "You've got a *bike?* That's a real beauty! Where did you get it?"

Tim threw aside his "surprise" as if it didn't matter. "Let go of her, Dad," he yelled. Rowdy and Cilla, startled by the roar, turned to look at their father. "Let go of her, I said!"

"What?" He looked down at his hand, which was clenching Jennifer's in a stranglehold. It was obvious who'd been doing the touching.

Then he looked at Tim, and an anger to match Tim's filled his soul. It was time he asserted the authority he'd lost more than three years before. If he kept living in the fear of Tim running away, their family would be ruled by the demands of an unwise, unstable eight-year-old.

When he spoke, it was with quiet authority that never failed to get through to his son. "I'm the grown-up here, Tim—you do as *I* tell you, not the other way around. What Jennifer and I do, or don't do, is between us alone. It isn't any of your business."

Tim's control slipped, seeming to shatter on the soft dirt footpath. *"You're married to my mum!"* he cried, his voice rising to the pitch of the small, terrified child he truly was.

Noah closed his eyes. The choice was as clear as it was heartbreaking. He either kept knuckling under to Tim's insecurity in the hope that his son would heal eventually, or he did what he could to give all three of his kids as normal a life as possible.

It was time to move on, whether Tim wanted to, or not.

He released Jennifer's hand and walked over to his son. When he reached Tim's side, he held his shoulders despite the boy's stiffening. "It wasn't me who left the family, Tim. Mummy went away because she was sad—but if she was coming home, she'd have come a long time ago. And all the yelling at me, and all the running away in the world, isn't going to bring her back to us. Do you understand, son? It's just us now."

"No. *No,*" Tim screamed, struggling against him, his face white. "She's coming home, she is. She *promised!*"

Noah's heart stalled at the terrible pain his son was in. "She promised to be home in an hour, matey," he said quietly.

Tim's little hands clenched into fists. "It's your fault! We shouldn't have left home!"

Noah closed his eyes for a moment, praying for inspiration, because his barrel had run dry. "She broke the promise three years ago, mate. She knew where we were all that time, and she never came home."

"You made her sad! That's why!"

Grimly he knew exactly who fed Tim that line. "I know Nana and Pa need to believe that—but it's not true, Tim." Noah faced his son without flinching. "Mummy was sick. She had something called post-natal depression, and she had it very badly. I didn't make her sad. I loved her—I'd loved Mummy since I was thirteen. I wanted her to come home. But the sickness got too much for her, the pills didn't help, and she ran away. But if she comes back to our old house, Nana and Pa live just down the road, right? She'll go there, and they'll tell her where we are."

"No, no!" Tim cried. His poor, thin little body was shaking; he didn't resist when Noah drew him into his arms, cuddling him close. "She can't, 'cause Nana and Pa aren't *there.*"

Noah frowned and pulled back. "What do you mean, Nana and Pa aren't there?"

"Get *away!*" Tim suddenly screamed, his face flushed with fury. "Get away from my dad!"

Noah turned and saw Jennifer a few feet away, her face filled only with tender sadness. "Tim, just this morning I was your friend. Just because I care about your dad too doesn't make me the enemy."

Noah's throat tightened with the words. *She does care about me.* He knew it, had known it all along—but hearing the words made it real somehow. Not just wanting, not mere fascination; she cared and he cared.

There was no going back now.

"Your dad was so scared about you, Tim. I hugged him to make him feel better. Can't I be your dad's friend, too?"

Tim turned from her, his thin face white and strained. The emotion so jumpy it was frightening. "Dad." The word was a plea—begging him to make a little boy's world secure again. To let him hang on to a faded thread of memory, the vow that was all he had left of his mother.

For a moment, Noah hovered on the brink of choice: giving in from pity as he'd done the past three years—or doing what he must to help Tim heal. Then he said quietly, "Tim, what did you mean about Nana and Pa not being home in Sydney?" But he knew exactly what Tim meant, and a grim sense of foreboding filled him. Peter and Jan would only leave home for one reason—the only reason for living they'd had from the day Belinda disappeared.

When Tim shuffled his feet, looking miserably guilty, Noah said it for him. "They're here, aren't they, mate? They heard about the lady who looks like Mummy. The one that lives here."

Tim looked up then, his eyes—eyes so like his mother's, despite the colouring being his—blazing. "You know about Mummy being here?"

Behind him, he almost felt Jennifer's body stiffen; but he had no time to reassure her. "Yes, matey, I know about the lady. Are Nana and Pa up here somewhere nearby?"

If they were, they wouldn't tell Noah. Though they'd known him all his life, and had been so joyful when he and Belinda married, they'd distanced themselves from him from the day the police marked her file Presumed Dead. When he'd accepted it rather than spending all his time and resources on finding her, their love had grown cold. When they called, they asked for Tim, who passed the phone to Cilla and Rowdy.

Suddenly he understood the reason for Tim's settling down the past few weeks. Peter and Jan had been feeding Tim from their unending well of hope.

"They're at a caravan park near Ballina," Tim said, his voice muffled against Noah's shoulder, shuffling his feet again. "They're looking for Mummy. They've been here a while."

Noah sighed. "I didn't tell them, but the police report about that lady was the original reason why we moved here, Tim. They showed me a photo, see. I didn't tell you all because I didn't want to get your hopes up, but the police told me there were sightings of a woman who looked a lot like her. I've been looking for her ever since we got here." He hesitated before he added, with painful difficulty, "About a year ago, I hired some special people who look for missing people for a living. They're looking for Mummy."

With that, Tim threw his arms around Noah's neck, burrowing close in a way he only had during nightmares for the past two years. The helmet he hadn't yet taken off whacked against Noah's collarbone. "Thank you, Dad," he whispered. "I was scared…"

*Scared you were forgetting Mummy.*

The words hovered like a spectre between them, the lie unspoken. For Noah knew now that even had the woman been Belinda, he would have tried to help her, reconciled her with the kids and Peter and Jan—but there was little left inside his own heart but memories. A month ago, he'd hired a second, local detective to find this woman, in a last-ditch effort to remember a marriage gone wrong, to stick to marriage vows long abandoned. The divorce papers he'd had the lawyer draw up last week were in his study now. The guilt and the shame and the relief all at once: ending a chapter of his life that seemed never-ending only three months ago.

But thanks to Jan and Peter's need to keep Belinda alive at all costs, his son's suffering just went on and on...

Was this why he'd seen the fear in his daughter's eyes? Why Cilla had been disappearing until they met Jennifer? *What the hell had Peter and Jan been telling his kids?*

It seemed today was the day for too many choices. This hour was an epiphany for them both. He could remain quiet, and let the pain come in its time and way, and have his son close again—or he could give Tim maximum anguish now, and let him find healing.

There really was no choice.

"I know Nana and Pa want Mummy to be alive as much as we do, but I heard from the special people last week. Remember the big letter you brought me?" he asked gruffly, hating to shatter his illusions even though he knew it was right. "They found the woman. Her name is Sandra Langtry, and she lives out in the bush with her partner and four kids. Though she looks a lot like her, she isn't Mummy—she had kids the same age as you and Cilla."

Tim's body went stiff for a few moments; then he gave a tiny cry, lost, soulless, like a dying animal. He broke out of Noah's hold and bolted for his wobbly bike.

And for once, Noah didn't even try to call him back.

As he disappeared down the road, a little hand slipped into Noah's. "We go in the car, Daddy?" Rowdy asked, helpfully. "We find Timmy?"

Noah looked down at his little boy, and a massive lump formed in his throat. Rowdy and Cilla were so completely un-affected by the news that their mother wasn't alive some-where nearby. It was as it should be, but it also seemed wrong

somehow, like he'd let the family down by not keeping
Belinda's memory alive and strong in them all.

As if healing was the disloyalty Belinda's parents believed it to be.

It was only now he'd begun to buck the system he'd per-
mitted Jan and Peter to create that he realised the damage he'd
done by allowing everyone to think Belinda *could* come home
after she'd been presumed dead. Tim was a child, and needed
to accept reality; he needed to begin the healing process at last.
He should never spend his time running: not running *away* as
he'd thought, but running around with his grandparents to find
his mum, who either couldn't or didn't want to come home.
And so his parents-in-law were going to find out before the
night was over.

No more status quo. It was time, not just to move on, but
to heal.

He watched Tim turn the bike left, toward the coast—
toward home, and sighed in relief. It seemed he'd been
right. Tim's disappearances had been about trying to find
Belinda—or, he thought grimly, to meet his grandparents.
"Yes, into the car—but we're going home, Rowdy. Timmy
needs time alone."

A risk he wouldn't have thought to take an hour ago now
seemed the only option. He couldn't stop Tim; his dream had
been shattered, his faith destroyed. He needed time out before
he'd accept his world needed to be reconstructed.

As Cilla and Rowdy, obedient as ever to following his
dictums on Tim, opened the truck doors to climb in, Noah
turned to Joe. "I'm sorry about all this."

To his shock, Joe was wiping tears from his cheeks. "No,
I'm sorry, son. I never realised—anyway, you might want to
call Fred and tell him Tim's safe," he said gruffly, trying to
recover from being caught out.

Noah nodded, and felt his pockets for his phone. Where had he put it after—

A voice said, sounding completely calm and in control, "I've called Fred already."

*Jennifer.*

The voice had come from inside the junkyard; she must have walked off to make the call.

Already knowing it was far too late, he turned to her. She was holding out his phone to him, with a tiny smile. "You dropped it when Tim came back."

She seemed unruffled. There was nothing on her face to indicate her emotional state. Nothing to gauge how she felt about his reasons for moving to Hinchliff—damn it, it must have sounded so *bad* to her, given what he'd said the first night about Belinda presumed dead—or about his kiss.

A one-moment brushing of lips. How did that qualify as a kiss in anyone's book?

*It does when nobody but a kid has touched you in years.*

A one-moment brushing of lips meant far more to him than it should, and with a sense of fatality, he knew that wouldn't change. He'd always been too intense. He'd never known how to play the field; for most of his life, his heart and body had focussed only ever on Belinda—then there'd been the years of nothing, where he'd been in limbo-land, over Belinda but not wanting anything with anyone but his kids.

And now the focus had returned: a tunnel-vision centred on Jennifer.

He'd have loved Belinda until his dying breath, if she was still here with him, loving him—and his fascination with Jennifer wouldn't change until then, either. He didn't know what his feelings were yet, but it had all the hallmarks of speeding-down-a-one-way-alley-into-a-wall he'd felt with Belinda all those years ago. He knew every curve and line of

Jennifer's face, what every movement of her mouth meant, how her eyes changed and darkened as her moods moved. He knew how she felt by the way she walked.

And he knew when she was in hiding. This time, her placidity was an act she'd put on to cover her pain—to seem stronger than she was. Why she'd begun this cover, he didn't know—yet—but he would find out.

He'd know everything about her, and soon.

"Thanks," he said quietly, allowing her to retreat while they were in company. He took the phone and pocketed it. "Let's get home."

He used the word *home* deliberately, testing her reaction, but she merely nodded. "The kids need their own home, and you need time on your own."

And though she smiled, she couldn't have been more distant from him if she'd climbed the crags overhanging the town behind Joe's house. She might have been talking of the weather, so light was her emotional investment. And somehow he just knew that spelled trouble.

## CHAPTER NINE

THEY headed for home as soon as Noah picked up the pizzas he'd ordered.

As they turned into the long driveway leading to her place, Jennifer knew her veneer of serenity was cracking, breaking open to show her vulnerability every time he looked at her, every time he spoke. She was surrendering to the needs of a body and heart too long buried beneath grief—and yes, the anger she couldn't totally bury, no matter how hard she tried.

And she was *hurt*...hurt that Noah had kissed her, awakening her body, only to—

*Oh, get over yourself. You've been into him from first sight. The kiss only made it real.*

*Don't think about it! Just bury the memory. You're good at that.*

Thinking about the rage and grief would lead her straight back to the pit she'd lived in too long after she'd buried her son. Acceptance and moving on was the only option.

"I'm sorry, Jennifer," Noah said, a welcome break into morbid thoughts she didn't want to indulge in. "I lied to you about why we moved here, and why I've been gone through the days. I wasn't always at work. I took advantage of your friendship to spend time looking for Belinda."

After a short breath, she turned to him. Barriers in place with a smile. "Don't apologise to me, Noah. It's not my place to know where you go or what you do. You did what you did for your family, for Tim. Never apologise to me for putting your kids first. I'd have done the same." She always had, with Cody.

"Thank you." But the words held a wryness that told her he wasn't buying it. He'd seen inside her soul, and the emotion she'd tried to hide.

She shrugged and twisted around to the kids. "Almost home."

"Are we going to your house, Jenny?" Rowdy asked, smiling through a mouth full of Hawaiian pizza.

She shook her head. "Not tonight, sweetie, but I'll see you tomorrow, okay? Daddy needs to get home for Tim."

Rowdy nodded, with his gift of accepting life as it was, and returned to making a mess of his clothes and the car seat with dripping mozzarella.

Cilla was trying to feed pizza to her new dolly: the gift Noah had probably bought to soften the blow that the woman he'd moved seven hundred kilometres to find wasn't their mother.

Jennifer frowned and turned back to Noah. "What was Tim's present?"

"A bike," he said quietly.

*Of course it was a bike,* she thought. Her life had become rich in irony since the Brannigans had moved in next door. It was as if she and Uncle Joe were here for the exclusive purpose of wrecking Noah's relationship with Tim.

"I'll keep it until his new bike breaks," he said with a casualness that really seemed genuine. "I'll offer him a trip to Coffs Harbour or Lismore, and he can pick whatever he wants. Within limits," he added with a laugh that again surprised her.

"You don't need to act with me," she said, taking the unspoken bull by the horns. "Surely you must feel some kind of grief or anger over the news about your wife?"

*Noah's wife. That's it, Jennifer, keep reminding yourself. Then the kiss will mean nothing to you but helping a scared dad who took comfort where it had been offered. Then you'll stop these ridiculous dreams of being Noah's love...Noah's wife.*

*Yeah, right—in about fifty years.*

He pulled up the truck at the side of her house, and turned to her, taking her hands in his. His eyes were dark, filled with emotion. "It's been over a week since I found out. I can't pretend there wasn't some kind of pain, Jennifer—but it wasn't the kind you're thinking. I—"

"Jen? Jen, is that you?"

The familiar voice wrenched her from the dreaming spell of Noah's sincerity, and his touch. She gasped; her eyes widened as the tall, strong figure came to the passenger side. She wrenched her hands from Noah's, and, as if in a dream, watched him opening the door. In the light of the new moon and the automatic spotlights on her verandah, she saw the features she'd once loved, dark, mysterious, romantic.

More irony, or was her life spinning out of control? "Mark?" Dazed, she stared up at the man who'd been her life and soul from the age of seventeen until the day he'd walked out on her when she'd needed him most. "Mark, what are you doing here?"

The Irish rogue's face—so like Cody's—lit up with a smile; those blue, blue eyes creased in the grin she could never resist, once upon a time. "Where else would I be on our tenth anniversary, but with my beautiful wife?"

He lifted her right up out of the passenger seat and pulled her into his arms, tipping her face up for his kiss.

Noah drove away from Jennifer's house, refusing to watch in the rearview mirror as she embraced the man who hadn't even noticed she'd been with another guy...

Was this Nature's joke on him? The day he realised there was no going back, the day he began to realise just how much Jennifer meant to him, her ex-husband shows up.

*No wonder she'd been acting strangely today. It's her wedding anniversary.*

So ended the belief that it was something he'd said or done that forced the change in her. She hadn't been thinking of him at all. So what if she liked his kiss? Any woman who hadn't seen her husband in a long time would be open to temptation.

*Ex-husband, Brannigan. And she asked why he was here. She didn't ask him to come.*

*She hadn't known Mark was coming.*

Did that mean—?

There were lights on in the house when he pulled up—and there was another car parked in the open garage.

A utility truck big enough to pull a caravan. The truck Peter and Jan had used the past three years to take a caravan to every place where there was a possible sighting of Belinda.

It seemed Tim had turned on his phone this afternoon, and made one call, at least. But wait—Tim hadn't had enough time to come home on his bike, call them and Peter and Jan to be here ahead of him. And that meant Tim either had their number on his phone, or he knew it off by heart.

He got the kids out of their seats, and took them inside.

It was after eleven when Noah finally saw Jennifer walking to him.

How he knew she'd come, he wasn't sure; they hadn't met here since that first night. Maybe it was his frantic hope that made it seem like belief. He only knew that, by God, he *needed* her, and she'd come.

He'd been waiting forty-five minutes, since Peter and Jan

finally left—only the lights on in her house fed his hope she'd be here.

If her ex-husband wasn't staying the night…

Then she was coming to him, like the miracle she'd always been.

Like the purple star-flowers, the white dress of summer was gone; in its place were jeans and a thick windcheater, since the nights had turned nippy in the past two weeks. Her feet crunched dried grass. As she drew closer, he turned the two-bar halogen lantern down to one bar, giving a soft half-light.

She looked as exhausted as he felt.

He held out a glass. "I was hoping you'd come."

"I wasn't sure," she said softly as she sank to the blanket. "I've been arguing with myself the past half hour."

His heart began pounding hard. Was she thinking of Mark? "Was it so hard?"

"I didn't want to make things worse for you and Tim," she said quietly.

"Belinda's parents were here tonight." Why he was telling her, he didn't know.

What a crock. Denial was useless when every pore and cell of him was beating in time to his heart, aching to touch her. He was taking her into his life. He was making her his woman.

"How did they take the news?"

He shrugged. "Badly, of course, but it wasn't as hard as I'd expected. Maybe because I had to confront them about them calling Tim, feeding him and Cilla, too, with their belief that she's alive and coming home soon…and that it was my fault she left. They told the kids I scared their mummy into running away." He blew out a frustrated sigh. "They've been damaging my kids in an effort to keep Belinda's memory alive."

"Oh, Noah." Her hand slipped into his, a natural gesture of comfort he cherished after thinking all night that he'd blown it with her. "No wonder Tim has been punishing you for trying to help him heal."

"And no wonder Cilla's been scared of me. I couldn't work it out." His head filled with her soft scent, the empathy brimming in her eyes, the feel of her work-roughened hand in his. The pretty, shimmering lips so *close.* "They picked a fight tonight in front of the kids. Tim told them about the private detective, and they wanted to know why I hadn't done it earlier. I had to tell them—" He stopped abruptly. There was a line between confidence and betrayal, and he'd been about to cross it. Not even to Jennifer could he say: *Belinda left me in so much damned debt I couldn't afford to pay a detective until a year ago.*

But Tim had heard it, and Noah knew he'd pay for that particular piece of impulsive anger for a long time to come.

And it had done no good. Peter and Jan refused to believe it. They clung to their picture of Belinda's perfection, and their bitter blaming of Noah, like it was their only lifeline.

Maybe it was.

"People believe what they want to, no matter how you show them the truth," she said softly. "Or maybe everyone's truth is different."

"They asked to take the kids away to the theme parks at the Gold Coast for a week," he said abruptly. Peter and Jan had *demanded* it, but they were the kids' grandparents, and God knew he needed a break right now. "They were devastated that the Langtry woman wasn't Belinda—and so is Tim. They all need time out, some fun. I'm sorry for the short notice."

A short silence. "It's all right."

"No, it isn't," he replied, his voice rough. "It's never damned fair the way they operate on guilt, but there isn't a bloody thing I can do to change it. They never listen to me anyway."

"As I said, people believe what they want to." Jennifer

walked into his thoughts as if she belonged in his head. "Look at my ex—a classic example. He's been gone three years, and he's been with several other women since he left me, but he was sure I'd take him back. Because I haven't been with another man, he thought it meant I still loved him."

She hadn't asked him to tell his secrets, but it didn't stop him asking. He had to know. "And you don't?"

Jennifer looked at him, and away. Her hand pulled from his before she spoke. "If you don't know the answer to that, you're blind."

The sudden acerbity in her tone didn't bother him. His heart beat even harder. "Feelings can come back when you see the person you once loved."

She wet her lips, breathing fast and shallow. "Is that what you believe of me, or yourself? If you moved here to be near her…"

"To *find* her," he corrected through a throat so damn tight with desire, it was choking him. "It was a last-ditch thing, mixed with desperation to get out of Sydney, the house we'd built together. My in-laws were making life a misery, but I had to let them see the kids. All they had left of her was the kids, and their unshakable faith that she's alive." He dragged in a breath before he made the confession, took the biggest personal risk of his life. "Then I saw you, and even from a distance, I knew I was in trouble."

The soft, glowing eyes turned back to him at last. She took in his face, slowly, every part of it. Her lips were already parted; her chest heaved with every breath. "I've never been the 'in trouble' kind of woman."

He smiled, a little. "Who's playing games now?" He moved closer to her, until the warm current of wanting grew to heat, fuelling their bodies.

She bit her lip over a grin: the kind of warm, sensuous curving of lips that told a man exactly what he needed to know. "This kind of game is…" Her tongue ran over her lips again, her gaze glued to his mouth. Her hand half-lifted, waiting in the middle of that hot, swirling current.

"Yeah," he breathed, lifting his hand, twining his fingers through hers. "It is."

"I can't do this if you're still married in your heart," she whispered.

He'd expected that. For answer he reached back with his free hand, and passed her the papers he'd signed. "I had to tell you before I sent them. It's for me, not you," he said quietly. "Meeting you made me see the truth. I can't hang onto something that's no more than a memory. Part of me will always love her…but she's gone. I can't keep living a half-life for Tim's sake, for my in-laws. Living a lie doesn't help anyone. It doesn't keep her alive, except in their minds."

She read the divorce papers, and closed her eyes as she let them fall. "This is why you bought the kids the presents."

He nodded.

She gave a little sigh. "Everything about us seems to have irony in there somehow. Is there a message in that?"

He leaned closer to her, and captured her other hand. "There's no timetable, Jennifer. There's no right time or way. It's happening, no matter what we do. We either ignore it and regret it later, or we take what we both want, and accept the consequences."

She looked at him, her eyes shimmering, uncertain. She wet her lips as she gazed at his face. He'd never felt so strong, so glad to be a man in his life as now, when Jennifer looked at him with all that longing.

"I want the consequences, Jennifer," he murmured huskily. "I want you. I want you."

"Noah." Her voice cracked; her eyes drifted closed, and she fell into him. "Don't make me wait anymore."

*Jennifer had waited for him.* Though he'd known it from the first night, he'd treasure the words until his dying breath.

Tender and a touch clumsy in first-kiss anxiety, they bumped each other's noses. He opened his eyes, drew back a little and smiled at her. Jennifer laughed, low and soft and throaty: a rich, sensuous laugh, and he knew she'd laugh just like that when they made love.

He unlaced their hands and twined his fingers through her loose plait. "Come here," he said huskily, drawing her against him.

For the first time in half a lifetime, the sense of fatality filling him was beautiful. He *knew* this would be the kiss of his life.

Holding her flush against him, he hovered just over her mouth, waiting, teasing, loving the impatient little moan coming from her, the way her hands threaded through his hair and drew him down to the blanket so he was half-lying on her.

She moaned again and moved against him. "Noah," she whispered, aching with wanting. She wanted him so badly she was shivering.

Then her mouth covered his, tender and hungry; and *rightness* filled his soul at the same moment his body's insistent beat took over everything and shut down every other sense.

The responses of her warm, generous body filled him with her sweetness and urgency. She kissed him gently, but when he took it deeper, she went with him; her hands were threading through his hair, fingers trailing down to his neck. The tiny, whisper-soft sighs between each kiss held a half-plea. "More, Noah…more…"

*More* was fine with him. Right now he never wanted to stop.

"So unfair," she whispered, more a tiny gasp of sound, as he kissed her throat.

He grinned down at her, a brow lifted. Her voice was so full of feminine arousal he knew it wasn't his kiss that was unfair.

Her smile in return was languorous. She pulled him back to her, and mock-grumbled between kisses, "The heatwave's over, and it's too cold to take your shirt off."

The fire burning in him flared higher, hotter. "Touch me all you want." Was that his voice? It sounded like tyres over gravel.

With a little sigh of delight, her hands slipped under his sweatshirt. "Ah, *Noah...*" She caressed him at first slow and soft, then with greater urgency, chest, stomach and waist; then she wrapped her arms around him and drew him back down to her. "More," she whispered.

When she said his name like that, said *more* like that, the thin threads of control snapped. He devoured her like a starving man at a feast, and she was with him all the way, whimpering and arching up to him with all the passion of his summer-hot dreams, and then some.

Touching, caressing with sweet discovery and wild tension; tongues twined and mouths fused. Loving had never been like this for him, never so intense yet so right and beautiful.

In his limited experience, men wanted the touch and play of lovemaking far more than women. Yet Jennifer's passion matched his, and raised the stakes. Her hands on his skin was making him crazy; the stroking of her tongue against the roof of his mouth short-wired every thought but the need to have her, now. Then one of her legs hooked around his, holding him down hard against her, and she moved against his aroused body again, her kiss hotter, deeper, almost frantic.

How had he been so *blind,* refusing to see what was right in front of him for so long? He thought he knew her; she'd reached right down to his soul from the start, not taking but *giving,* and he'd been drowning in her understated beauty and quiet grace from the first night.

*Jennifer.* Even the name had become beautiful to him.

But this Jennifer was vivid, passionate, raw with desire.

She was melting into him like candle wax, making soft, eager sounds, her fingers and palms not just caressing his skin, but gulping it down, as hungry for him as he was for her. Mumbling his name between kisses and touches so *glorious* he lost all sense of time and place. Nothing else in his life had ever been like this. *Jennifer, Jennifer...*

He must have said it aloud, because she pulled back to smile, glowing with happiness and desire. "Noah, oh, yes, Noah," she mumbled, and tugged at him until he was lying fully on top of her—and his brain circuits sizzled. "More, more."

Oh, man, but he loved that word...

He smiled, but she'd pulled him back down before he could speak. More kisses, mouth, throat and at the vee of his sweatshirt. "I had to throw him out," she mumbled, rolling them over until she lay on him. "He touched me, kissed me, and I just wanted him to go away." She kissed him all over his face, throat, chest. His placid, everyday Jennifer seemed taken over by another being, a wild woman with no thought beyond touching him, loving his body. "He wasn't you, Noah, he wasn't you."

The kiss following her words was even hotter, filled with a need so strong—not a need for any man, but him alone—it knocked him for six.

Torn between masculine triumph at her confession and primitive fury that another man touched her, he growled between kisses on her throat, "Did you tell him about us?"

Suddenly she stilled. "How could I? There was nothing to tell."

He lifted his head and looked down at her, flushed and drugged with his kisses—and just a touch wary. "There is now. Is he still in town?"

The wild passion in her banked down, like a fire after someone stomped on it. She nodded. "He said he'd stay a few days to see if I'd change my mind."

Another irony in their relationship—he'd gone crazy trying to find his wife for three years; she had her ex back and didn't want him. "When he comes back, tell him about us."

"And say what?" she asked with the fierceness of passion thwarted. He wished he'd kept his mouth shut—or kept speaking the language she'd been loving so much. "That we can't keep our hands off each other, despite knowing we have no future? That stolen hours at a café, or meeting on a blanket in the grass in the night fifty feet from your kids is all we can have, but we take it anyway?" She pushed off him and rolled away.

Put with such blunt ferocity, he stared at her, a slow frown gathering between his brows. "Is that what you think? That I'd use you that way after all you've done for me, for the kids?"

"Did I say it was just you?" she snapped. "I've been just as stupid. I *told* you I had my reasons for staying out of this, yet here I am."

"This." She'd called it "This," as if kissing and touching him was a disease she'd tried to avoid by washing her hands. "I remember," he said grimly. "So why did you come tonight?"

Her eyes met his with quiet defiance. "You know why. I'm not going to lie for the sake of some misplaced pride. I'm here because I couldn't think about anything else after you kissed me today. But there's no future for us. You're not divorced, you're not a widower…and I'm—"

"I showed you the papers. I'll be divorced in a month or two. I'm not using you, Jennifer."

She gave a choked laugh. "That's really not the point, is it?"

"Then what is?" But he knew. "Jennifer, I'm not playing here. I want you in my life, not just in bed. I want you, not a baby!"

"But I do, Noah."

In the grip of fury greater than any he'd felt in years, he snapped, "So you're saying I'm not enough for you? My kids aren't enough?"

"You don't understand. It's *me*. It's not just a wish, Noah—it's a bone-deep part of me I can't change. I can't allow myself to fall in love with you—I'll only make you all miserable in the end. Your kids deserve better than the second-best love I can give them...*you* deserve better than a woman who can't give you children, but will never stop wanting them." With a sigh, she got to her feet. "I shouldn't have come here. I'm sorry. There's just too many people who can be hurt. Even if you wanted something serious with me, it's not going to happen. I won't let it."

Noah watched her walk away, her stride swift and determined. She meant every word of what she said.

## CHAPTER TEN

JENNIFER knew something was wrong when Noah showed up late the next morning—just before the other kids and parents arrived—and alone. With a brief "good morning, Jennifer," he taped up the west-facing windows.

"Where are the kids?" she asked, frowning.

"With their grandparents—remember? I told you last night," he replied. "Excuse me. I'm starting the actual building today, as you know, so I'll be putting the barricades up to block the kids from coming in." He turned and walked out the door.

She followed him out, too angry to think. "And that's it? You turn up late, don't even bring the kids to say goodbye—"

He just kept walking. "The kids needed time out, away from here."

That silenced her for a few moments. "I see," she said eventually. They were alone…

Burning heat flashed across her cheeks. As if she floated in the sky above them the night before, she saw them entwined on the blanket, kissing as if it were the last night on earth…

The look he threw at her held a tamped-down fire of warning. "There's no other sightings of Belinda left to follow," he said quietly. "Peter and Jan are pretty devastated."

The flat statement broke into her sensuous visions of last

night, and made her take a step back. "Of course," she faltered, feeling as if she was the one in the wrong, and he'd deliberately put her there. "I'll miss them."

"When they come home, I'll be making other arrangements for them." His voice was as hard as the dark wood he was using for the verandah.

Now she really gasped. "Would you mind telling me why?"

He wouldn't even look at her; he put the barricades in place between them, winding the orange cross-over plastic across the posts. "I thank you for all your kindness until now—but I can't let you hurt them."

The words came across the plastic as if it was an abyss…and she knew whatever he said next, she'd hate it; but she couldn't walk away.

"They love you," he remarked casually, as if it meant nothing. "Cilla and Rowdy think of you as a mother. Even Tim adores you and looks to you for security—and as you said last night, you won't even think about it. You say you can't love them as they deserve." He moved away, winding more plastic across the next pole. "They've already lost one mother. I have to separate you from them before it gets any worse."

A shaking hand lifted to her mouth. "I—Noah, I—"

But he shook his head. "Excuse me. I need to work now."

His cool politeness was a barrier higher than any he created physically.

Within a minute he was bent over the lathe, cutting a verandah plank to the right length.

And Jennifer turned and walked back into the house, to greet the children arriving—children she loved, but weren't her heart, just work, and she was filled with a sense of loss so profound she couldn't argue, couldn't even speak.

Damaged, loving Tim. Adorable Cilla. Beautiful, trusting Rowdy. And *Noah*…

She'd made the decision; it was the best thing for them all—but she hadn't counted on losing them all so soon. She felt as if she'd lost her family a second time over.

The lights were still on at Jennifer's house.

Noah sat at his back verandah, watching a blur of a shadow pass from room to room, which was all he could see at this distance. Lost without the kids to fill his evenings, more alone than he'd ever been, he watched her house, watched her and hated himself. He'd only done what he'd had to do, but he felt lower than a snake's belly for hurting her.

Regrets were useless. It was over. Jennifer's decision left him with no choice. He had to get the kids away from her before it got any worse for them; but he had to fight himself just to keep sitting here, to not go over there, to take her in his arms and comfort her, kiss her until—

His kids had to come first. He could risk his heart, but not the kids'. Not after losing one mother.

Decision made—but it didn't stop the savage argument inside him. He loved the woman so damned *much.* Heart and soul, he belonged to her, to Jennifer—and she didn't want him. Not for life. And that was all he could offer. He wanted forever, could offer nothing but forever, and she didn't want it.

*She does want it,* his heart whispered. *She's just terrified she isn't enough. She's blinded herself to all that's wonderful about her because she can't have babies.*

The sudden insight didn't shock him. Maybe he'd known it all along. Jennifer thought it was about that *bone-deep* desire for her own babies—but he knew how much she loved his kids. She was a natural-born mother who hadn't yet come to terms with her loss. He had to show her…to open her mind and heart to new possibilities…

He was at her door before he realised he'd made the decision, or even how he'd convince her. He only knew he had to try.

A soft Elvis ballad was playing on the CD player. Scented candles were lit around the house, as if she expected a lover; but through the screen, he could see her bent over the kitchen sink. Her arms were wrapped tight around her waist; her body heaved and rocked, and she was crying as though her heart had been ripped from her chest.

"Jennifer!"

By the time she gasped and whirled around, trying to wipe her cheeks, she was in his arms. "Ah, baby, don't cry," he growled. "I can't stand it."

Half expecting her to stand stiff and cold in his embrace, or to pull away, he felt her arms wrap around his waist with a surge of joy so strong it was almost pain. "Noah. *Noah.*" The whisper was harsh, violent in need. She hiccupped, gulped down air, and hiccupped again.

He tipped up her face, kissing her wet cheeks, damp eyes, her mouth. "I know, baby, I know." He kissed her again, drinking in each hiccup of grief, giving her the affection and comfort she needed. "It's just you and me. I'm here, Jennifer. I'm here."

Her arms lifted, wrapping around his neck, and winding into his hair…and she kissed him, heartfelt kisses that lasted forever, promised forever, her red-rimmed, swollen eyes taking him in with a look of wonder, as if he'd vanish if she turned away.

She'd never looked more beautiful to him. He knew what he meant to her; she couldn't hide it, not now, vulnerable in her grief for losing him—*him,* not just the kids. If she wasn't in love with him, she was more than halfway there.

But love wasn't the issue; they both knew that.

It wasn't the time to push—but he could make a start. "I sent the papers today. I know that's not the problem," he added, when she stiffened and began to speak. "I don't think we're going to see the real issues clearly until we've spent time together alone. We've had nothing but problems and issues and kids since we met, Jennifer. The past has affected us both too much."

"I know," she whispered, holding him tight. "I've hated that."

"Me, too…but for now it's just you and me, and we have a week. Let's take the time we have. No promises, no issues—let's be just you and me, doing what we want, for once."

Her eyes were so uncertain. Unsure of what he wanted.

He smiled a little. "No, we won't make love—not yet. I want the right to take you out for dinner, for a ride—I haven't taken my motorbike out since we moved here."

"I didn't know you had one." She smiled up at him.

"With two helmets. Are you afraid of riding?"

"I've never done it, but always wanted to try."

"Come with me tomorrow," he whispered, rough and hard-edged with desire, trying to keep it down. "We'll go to the escarpment at the national park after work. No—let's play hooky. Fridays you usually only have my kids, right? So you have tomorrow off. Let's spend the day together, just you and me."

Jennifer didn't even hesitate. She nodded, her eyes shining.

"I want to spend time with you without worrying about anything else." The gravelly tone of his voice almost scared him. This meant so damned much, and she was glowing, her eyes drinking in his face as if he was beyond special to her. "Just you and me."

"For this week, until the kids come home," she whispered back.

She meant to reassure him, but it only sent scalding pain searing through his entire body. He nodded, not trusting his voice.

"I looked up other child-care centres in the area for you this afternoon. There's three in Ballina, and one at Everwood. That's only fifteen minutes from here."

The shock of it hit him harder than it should have. Being Jennifer, of course she'd try to help him, even if it meant losing the kids she adored. "Thank you," he said quietly; but the night-magic was gone. He pulled out of her arms. "I'll pick you up about ten. Bring a thick jacket."

The anxiety was back in her eyes, but she nodded. "I'm looking forward to it. I always thought I'd feel—dangerous—riding on the back of a motorbike."

Despite the pain, he chuckled and buffed her chin. "You're dangerous enough as it is. Don't get ideas."

"Me? Dangerous?" she laughed, catching his fist in her hand and caressing it. "Nobody's ever called me that before."

"Then they didn't know you," he muttered. His renegade body was getting ideas of its own, just feeling the repressed sensuality in her caress.

"Dangerous. I like it." She grinned at him, and brushed his body with hers. "I like it a lot." Her voice was all gentle and husky, filled with promise.

If he stayed here any longer, he'd end up in her bed. He knew he could make her want it, here and now—she already did. But he was in way too deep. If he made love to her now, he'd want things she wasn't ready to give. He had to wait. An old-fashioned courtship was the surest way to make her see they belonged together—that they could surmount the difficulties she saw as impossible. Yet right now he'd give anything just to touch her, drink in her bare skin with his hands and mouth…

"You're too dangerous for my peace of mind." His voice was all rough-edged and tight. "I'd better go."

"You don't have to," the voice of temptation whispered into his neck.

He felt the shudder rock his whole frame. "Stop it," he

growled, aiming for a joking tone that failed miserably. "We have a week. I'm going to do this right."

"At least one date before—"

"Don't say it, Jennifer. I'm on the edge as it is."

Her laughing tone died; she looked up at him, saw the truth of his words, and smiled. "I'm so glad it's not just me that's on the edge. I'm beginning to wonder if I'll ever think about anything else but wanting you." She kissed his shoulder through the thick woollen jumper, and he shuddered again. "See you tomorrow."

She swatted his butt with a grin as he headed for the door. He grinned back at her. "I'll get you for that, woman."

"I hope so," Jennifer whispered as she watched him leap over the boundary fence. Her knees were weak, and her body was flushed and tense with the need for him she couldn't fight, much as she wanted to—no, *had* to.

For Noah's sake, and for the kids, she could have him only for this week. She'd make love to him, and then she'd let him go.

He roared up to her back doorstep just before ten the next morning, looking like pure sin in the dark jeans, boots and black leather jacket. He flipped up the visor, grinned and held out a helmet. "Ready?"

She caught her breath back and even managed an unsteady laugh. "You bet. Where are we going?"

With a wink, he said, "You'll see." He looked her over, taking in the jeans and joggers with approval, but frowned at her long-sleeved pink T-shirt. "You'll be cold during the ride." Reaching into the black container at the back, he pulled out a jacket almost identical to his.

Jennifer flinched.

"It's my old jacket from uni days," he said as if he hadn't

seen or noticed that she'd obviously thought it was Belinda's jacket. "See the old political patches?"

She saw, and slowly smiled, seeing a young, renegade Noah on his motorbike…

"Feeling dangerous still?"

She pulled it on, zipped it up and challenged, "Well?"

"Let's go." He moved forward on the seat. She hopped on, fitted the helmet and wrapped her arms around his waist, almost unbearably excited. Her first real date in ten years or more, and he'd made it her deepest secret fantasy without even trying.

"Hold on tight," he yelled, and roared off. Feeling like a girl again, she squealed and held on tighter to him, loving that she had the right—for now.

They flew through Hinchliff, leaving indignant residents in their wake. Jennifer couldn't stop laughing. After years of a humdrum existence, she was a woman again, and she'd snatch every moment of it she could.

Hitting the highway, he headed north, weaving through traffic with easy skill. Jennifer waved at all the kids who waved at them; she grinned at the women staring in envy. Lord knows, she used to feel envy at the glorious freedom of the bikers. She shivered. Until today—until Noah came into her life, she hadn't known she'd been walking around half-dead. She was living now, really living…she was living out a dream with the man of her dreams. Who could argue with her happiness?

"Cold?" he yelled over the thunderous noise of the engine beneath them.

"No! It's wonderful!"

She felt the rumble of laughter shake his frame, and smiled back, even though he couldn't see it. Who cared if she was being a Pollyanna? The feel of his body surrounding her was enough to make her smile for years to come.

They flashed along the highway, with deep bush each side until it seemed to burst into clean lines of sand and the beach on one side, and tall, dark hills on the other. He roared off to the left, up the darkened road through steep hills covered in gum trees and tangled undergrowth.

In her two years in Hinchliff, she'd never been up this way. "What's up here?" she yelled.

"You'll see." He geared down, and the engine became even louder—and she loved it. The cool, clean air, the dark forest, the feeling of mystery and adventure in not knowing where she was going with Noah—just being with him, without others around to monitor them…having fun without counting the cost.

Oh, yes, this was the stuff of dreams. She almost felt young again. She felt *happy*.

At the top of the hills—a crest far back from the first hill—he finally pulled up.

Jennifer hopped off the bike and pulled off her helmet, her eyes wide with delight. "What is this place?"

Noah grinned at her. "You like it?"

"Definitely." Shining-eyed, she turned in a slow circle. The street was cool and shady, seeming almost a part of the forest surrounding it. The houses and stores were in dark wood, looking both pretty and yet ancient. "Where are we?"

"Lindenbrook. It's a heritage-listed town. It was first built around 1902. They say some famous bushranger started the place as his cover. He ran a store when he wasn't bushranging—or maybe his lady did."

"How did you find it?" She was still turning round and round, taking in the old wooden park, the Hollywood-cinema era café, the quilting store.

Her eyes lit up.

Noah laughed, and turned to chain the bike and helmets together. "I thought you'd want to have a look in there. Their range is more extensive than you'd think. I nearly bought you some stuff last time I was here, but the lady convinced me I'd probably buy the wrong stuff for you—she said quilters can be pretty choosy about what they want."

She noticed he'd avoided answering her question about how he'd found the place—and after a moment she knew why. She didn't ask a second time. Why ruin the day with references to his search for his missing wife?

"Do you still want the jacket?" he asked, in the quiet tone that told her she was right. He wanted to forget—and so did she—about anything that reminded them their time together would be too brief for them both.

She shook her head, and unzipped the jacket, holding it out to him. "Have I got helmet hair?"

"Shake it out a bit." He came to her, minus his jacket—wearing a collarless long-sleeved shirt in the colour of storm clouds. "Let me." His hands threaded through her plait, loosening it until the band fell out and her hair tumbled around her shoulders in loose waves. "Much better," he said softly, his eyes deep and dark. Then he kissed her, long, sweet and gentle.

She almost melted into a puddle at his feet. Her hands gripped his shoulders. "More."

"I love that word when you say it," he whispered against her mouth and kissed her again, still with the tenderness that left her a shivering pool of heat and joy.

"Coffee? Tea? *Anything?*" he asked long minutes later, in a taut, hot voice that told her he was close to losing control, out here in a public street.

Without a word, she nodded.

He wrapped his arm around her, putting her arm around his waist, and led her to the café, in the quiet of wanting too much. Afraid one word would break the constraints they'd agreed to.

They had hot chocolate in a shadowed corner, and discovered how it tasted to sip chocolate from each other's mouths; talking inbetween, about their lives and ambitions, about the verandah's progress—nothing that led to awkward silence. She confessed her fascination with old thirties movies; he liked Jackie Chan. She liked romantic novels; he enjoyed biographies and sci-fi. He loved doing up old houses, and planned to make it a major part of his new business, especially since that was fast becoming the number-one query he was receiving from clients.

He'd also found to his surprise that he loved living in Hinchliff. For a city boy, he'd discovered the love of quiet, and he never wanted to go back. "Dural's pretty quiet, anyway. It's a place with acreages everywhere, so it's got the small-town feel, while being close to the city."

She nodded. "It's similar in Swansea. It's small suburbia, half an hour or more from Newcastle. I could never live right in a city. I like knowing most people in the area, and who the local policeman is."

They talked until they were interrupted. "Did you want to order anything else? Another hot chocolate, or maybe lunch?" the waitress asked, smiling as she came toward them.

Noah checked his watch, and his brows lifted. "It's after twelve-thirty." He looked at Jennifer. "What do you want to do? The gourmet pizzas here are pretty sensational."

Surprised to discover she was hungry, she nodded.

"It will take about twenty minutes. Want to go visit the craft and quilting store?"

Her hand was in his already as she rose to her feet.

The quilting store was one of those curio kinds of stores that hold a bit of everything that Jennifer adored. She wandered around twice, and found one or two items she'd been after for a long time. She took them to the counter with a massive smile of pride and happiness; but Noah had already pulled out his card when she reached for her purse. In his hand was the item she always lost: a thimble. In fact he had half a dozen of them. He grinned and winked and she felt the blush touch her cheeks. He knew why she'd stabbed her finger so often…

"Put them all on one purchase," he told the woman behind the counter. His tone told Jennifer he'd brook no denial on this. He was in charge today.

It felt good to be cherished.

While they wandered back to the café, Jennifer suddenly wanted to tell him something. "I sent Mark back to Newcastle yesterday."

Noah's arm tightened around her waist. He turned her around to face him. "Did you tell him about me?"

She laid a hand on his chest. "I told him there was a stubborn man next door with three adorable kids who made going back to him impossible." She smiled and shrugged. "Not that he really wanted it, anyway. I think he was at a loose end between women, and thought he'd get taken care of for a while. Until he was ready to leave, of course."

"I doubt that—" Noah stopped as he thought about her words. There was something…he frowned as he realised. She'd told her ex about him yesterday—before he came to her last night. She'd told Mark about him, even when he'd made it clear he was cutting her out of their lives.

For the first time, hope soared inside him. Did this mean she wanted him beyond this week? To toss her ex out of her life for him, within hours of his ending all connection with her—

"Noah?"

He kissed her: a butterfly kiss, but he felt her quiver and drag in a breath. "I'm glad you feel like that," he growled. Now wasn't the right time to say everything in his heart. She wasn't ready yet. She'd show him in her time and way. He had to believe that, because she'd taken him body, heart and soul. Giving her up wasn't an option anymore, even for the kids. Whatever Tim thought he wanted, all three of his kids needed Jennifer almost as much as he did.

Now he had to make her want a life with him more than her longing for a baby of her own—more than her fears of inadequacy.

The words were out before he'd thought it through. "Tell me what Mark said to make you feel as if you wouldn't be good enough for me and the kids."

# CHAPTER ELEVEN

JENNIFER stared at him. "What?" *Mark?* He actually thought—

She frowned and pulled away from him, feeling bewildered and betrayed. "You couldn't even wait four hours, could you? I thought we were supposed to just enjoy the day, to enjoy our week together. But you're pushing for what I've already told you is impossible!"

The waitress arrived at the doorway, looking for them at that moment. "Your lunch is ready," she called, with a smile.

They walked back to the café, but without the tender connection of earlier—and she found herself grieving for what she'd only had for a few hours. He'd promised her a week...

The waitress put the steaming pizza on their table, along with their cutlery and plates. "Enjoy, folks. Would you like something to drink with that? Some sparkling apple juice, or ginger ale, or cold water?"

"No, thanks." Though Noah smiled up at the woman, he had that repressed intensity about him again. The moment she was gone he turned back to her, his eyes burning. "Tell me, Jennifer. Tell me what he said that's so important that you'd destroy our chance at a life together."

Denial was useless at this point; Noah knew she wanted to be with him. She wasn't the kind of woman to play around. She'd never have kissed him, touched him or offered to make love, if her heart wasn't deeply involved. "It wasn't Mark. It was never Mark." She could feel the shaking begin, deep inside. "He didn't care about having more kids. He didn't care about my defect. The only reason he left me was because I put Cody before him, and he couldn't stand the constant sickness." She lifted a slice of pizza onto her plate. "He tried to come back to me after Cody—he couldn't understand why I didn't joyfully welcome him back. He loved me, he said—he just didn't want to come second, even for his sick three-year-old son. He was glad I wouldn't have more kids!"

After a long silence, Noah said, "Don't despise him for hiding from the truth, Jennifer—or for not knowing you. He probably loved you in his way—he just wasn't mature enough to want to put Cody first. Sometimes it's easier to ignore stressful situations, to let someone else deal with them, or to run away, than stay and face the fact that you have to make changes in your life."

The unwilling empathy in his tone took her aback. "Did you run from Belinda? I can't believe you'd ever leave your kids."

He gave her a small half smile. "Thanks for the faith, but there are many ways to run without leaving physically. I only learned to stop hiding my head in the sand when it was too late. I only grew up when I was left alone with three pre-schoolers and a mountain of debt I couldn't even work off, because I had to stay home with the kids. It was only then I realised that though I'd always loved her, I loved the vision I had of her when we were kids, and when we were first married. I didn't want to face how deep her depression was because it didn't fit the way I wanted her to be."

"That's why you didn't divorce her until now, isn't it?" she asked slowly.

He shrugged. "There's a bucket load of guilt in every direction I look. Things started getting bad for us when she fell pregnant with Rowdy. She didn't want another child so soon after Cilla. When she mentioned abortion, I took it personally instead of seeing it as a cry for help. She was a fantastic mother, and I couldn't see that she wouldn't cope with three as well as two. She did everything for the kids, and I worked to pay the bills. I thought it was how things should be." His face tightened. "I blinded myself to every sign of her depression because, to me, it meant I was going wrong, or I'd have to change something about me to make her happy."

"Is that why your in-laws blamed you for her disappearance?"

"They had to know I was in denial. Belinda called her mother every day, and took the kids to visit three times a week. They would've known more than I did about her feelings, because I didn't listen. I didn't want to know."

She looked in his eyes, and instead of self-recrimination, she saw determination, and hidden purpose. "Why are you telling me this now?"

His eyes remained steady on her face. "So you know the truth about me. I'm no prize. I'll make more mistakes. You saw enough of them at the start. I was falling down when we met—without you and Joe I don't know where I'd be now, let alone the kids." He gathered her hands back in his. "But that's not the reason I want a life with you. You know it isn't." His eyes were dark, intense on hers. "Marry me, Jennifer. Not for the kids, not because I need you, but because you want to spend the rest of your life with me. Because you love me as much as I love you."

The shaking went right down to her bones; tears filled her eyes, and she couldn't breathe. Dream and nightmare met and kissed, and temptation and desperate fear clawed right through her. "I can't, I just can't," she babbled. "I'm sorry, but I told you I couldn't."

Noah didn't seem to be insulted, hurt or even taken aback. "That was a bit sudden, wasn't it?" he asked, with a rueful smile. "I was going to ask at the end of the week."

Unsteadily she replied, "My answer will be the same, now or then."

"Are you saying you don't love me?" he asked, the quiet tone in no way hiding the demand; but she didn't know how she felt about anything right now, except that she couldn't marry him. Helplessly she shook her head.

"Do you know how you feel?" he asked, his gaze on her face: all her turbulent confusion must be very obvious. "I think you do care, Jennifer. I think you're afraid to look at your feelings because it might hurt you too much."

"I told you why I wouldn't marry again," she mumbled, blinking hard, trying to hold in the tears. She hadn't shed a tear since coming to Hinchliff…until an open-hearted man with three adorable kids walked in her back door, and she felt as if she'd been crying ever since.

"You said you wouldn't marry for the kids—or for love, because if you loved a man, you'd want his baby," he said softly, his gaze holding hers. "Do you want my baby, Jennifer?"

*Yes! Yes! More than anything in the world!*

She gulped the massive hardness in her throat as the truth knocked her silly. The question, and her unconscious answer, made her see the truth far more than his flat-out demand to know if she loved him a minute before.

*Love.* She'd loved him all along, probably from the first day—but she'd refused to acknowledge it because this moment would always be inevitable, ready to destroy her fragile illusions of control. Because grief was crouching, ready to pounce on her like the monster under the bed that woke her at night when she was little.

Because denial was the only hold on sanity she had.

She loved him more than she'd ever thought to love any man, and she adored his children. She loved them almost as much as she'd loved Cody…

Could it work? Could she make them all happy with *almost?* Could she mother his children and not long for more—or would she eventually hurt them all with what she couldn't change?

How could *almost* be good enough? This beautiful family deserved so much better than second best…and if he touched her now, if he said he loved her again, she'd—

*Break.*

The word she'd overheard Uncle Joe use that night, talking to Noah, was more appropriate than she'd have admitted only a week ago. Joe knew her too well; he knew this meant too much.

Because Noah and his beautiful kids had become her world, and that terrified her.

"Jennifer?" His voice, so tender and understanding, walked into her mind, soothing the turmoil just by being there. "It's not as impossible as you think. We can work this out."

She couldn't speak; she just shook her head. Some things couldn't be sorted out.

"Think about it, Jennifer. Why can't this work for all of us? Why isn't love enough? I know you love me, and you *do* love the kids."

Think? There was nothing to think about, but loving Noah and losing him. Yes, she loved his kids, but not as they deserved…they deserved a *mother,* not a woman giving them second-best love, making them a substitute for her own children…

\* \* \*

Watching her white face and blank, horrified eyes, he pushed aside the uneaten pizza. He'd blown it. Why hadn't he waited? If he'd given her a week—

He hadn't known quite what to expect when he'd asked her about having his baby, but the look on her face left him speechless—the anguished longing and devastation combined.

Too late, he knew this was something she'd always feel utterly alone with, just as he'd felt about Belinda's disappearance. He could never fully understand her loss, having fathered three healthy children with ease.

He should have *thought* before he'd blundered in. Jennifer did nothing but give to him, and he'd thrown her impossible dream in her face as though he could make a miracle happen.

The look on her face had said it all. Jennifer loved him, far deeper than she'd shown him until that moment. He knew it now, just as she knew. She loved his kids, and they adored her.

No, love wasn't the issue.

Acceptance was the real, core issue: Tim needed to accept his mother was gone, but the most incredible substitute already loved him, and the whole family. Jennifer had already accepted she couldn't have the one dream of her life…but she'd blinded herself to a love that would be there for her for the rest of her life. She couldn't see that the kind of love they shared was more than enough for them all.

They could become a family, if only she'd let it happen.

Changing a lifetime of thinking didn't occur in an hour. He'd been a fool to bowl on in like that; but love and longing overcame good sense. Not needing her so much as wanting to make her happy, his beautiful, giving Jennifer.

He opened his mouth to say something to soothe the moment, to give her space and time. Then his phone bleeped—and he went cold. The bleeping sound was what he'd programmed for the police. Tim—Cilla—Rowdy—

He flipped the phone open. "Fred," he greeted the sergeant tersely. "What is it? The kids?"

What he heard made him go cold all over.

She despised herself…but how could she change the person she was?

Lost in her thoughts, she'd vaguely realised Noah was on the phone to someone, and turned away to give him privacy.

Not thinking wasn't an option, unless she gave herself amnesia—which sounded really tempting right now. To be able to forget all this pain…

*You want to forget Noah? Forget the kids?*

She knew she would never do that even if she could. The Brannigan family had changed her placid, uneventful, boring life forever. They'd challenged her, made her think and act in ways that she hadn't known were part of her. They'd needed her so much, yet she'd been given so much more than she'd given to them. And Noah—

She closed her eyes, fighting the emotion threatening to overcome her. If only—

"Jennifer."

The shock in Noah's tone jerked her out of her thoughts. "Noah?" She looked up, shocked by his white face and blank, cold eyes. "What is it? Are the kids all right?"

He took his time answering, but it wasn't deliberate. She wondered if he'd even heard her. Finally he spoke, slow, jerky—lost. "They've found Belinda."

The ride back was tense and silent.

Noah felt physically ill. He didn't know what to say to her after that one sentence. What else *was* there to say? He didn't know anything else. Fred had said, "There's been a positive identification this time, Noah. They've found your wife. I can't say more on the phone—I wasn't supposed to say that much, but I wanted you to be prepared. The Sydney people are here, but I convinced them to let me handle it first. I'll be waiting at your place with all the details."

*They've found your wife.*

The words he'd prayed so long and hard to hear, given in the same hour he'd proposed to Jennifer. When else would it happen?

Jennifer was barely holding on to him, her hands on his waist instead of around his chest as they'd been this morning. A minimal touch—just as she'd touch him if he were another woman's husband…

*What if he was?*

He almost threw up at the thought. Oh, he'd be happy for her, for Peter and Jan and the kids; but though he was still fond of Belinda, he wasn't the same man-child he'd been only three years ago. He'd grown up, and his heart changed with him—and now he'd given it to Jennifer.

But if Belinda was alive, and wanted their marriage and family back, he knew Jennifer would quietly withdraw, and disappear from his life.

Yet somehow he felt sure his wife wasn't alive. Peter and Jan's faith was the desperate blindness of parents who can't face outliving their beloved daughter, and they'd passed it on to Tim. But Noah had always known. If there was one thing he knew about Belinda, it was that she'd never have left her kids.

*She wouldn't have left me either—not without a word.*

They'd had their troubles, but he and Belinda had said "I love you" to each other the morning she'd disappeared. Tim's testimony to the tender kiss between his parents—a ritual he'd seen every day—had slowed the momentum on police suspicions. He supposed the lack of evidence, and no other woman in his life, had helped as well.

It was almost in shock that he found himself pulling up outside his house. Lost in the past—in the final, tenuous links to his life with Belinda, apart from the kids—he'd ridden almost an hour without a word to Jennifer.

Her face, when she pulled off the helmet, was white—as if she'd been fighting the same sickness he had. "Jennifer—"

"Fred's waiting," she said softly.

"Come inside with me." He spoke with a desperation he couldn't hold in. "I need you."

Her face slightly averted, she nodded, making a motion with her hand for him to go first.

Fred's lined, honest face looked grim and sad, and Noah knew what he had to say before he said it.

"She's dead, isn't she, Fred?" The words were so damn flat. No emotional investment at all. Why was that, when suddenly he felt something breaking inside him?

Fred said, with a flicked glance at Jennifer, "Let's go inside, Noah. There's a lot to say."

Jennifer followed the men in without a word or expression. She seemed to drift in, like a small boat listing on a river without its anchor, and sat at the other end of his long, wide living room, her gaze out the window.

She couldn't have stated her protest at being here more clearly if she'd shouted it; but he didn't let her off the hook and tell her to go. Whether she liked it or not she had an emotional investment in this.

Though he'd sat, Fred was twisting his hat in his hands. He looked at Noah, and away. "Yes, she's dead. I'm sorry, Noah. They found her body a couple of weeks ago, but had to get definite DNA evidence to prove it was your wife."

Translation: *the body was too decomposed to be sure…*

Noah's head fell; his voice sounded strange even to his own ears. "Where was she found? Why did they think it was Belinda in the first place? Did—did she leave a letter?" The unspoken question hovered in the air. *Did she kill herself? Did she hate her life that badly?*

"No, she didn't." Fred sighed. "They were sent an anonymous letter by the person who killed her. The dates given and the locale made them pretty sure they'd find your wife."

His head shot back up so fast it hurt his neck. Vaguely he felt Jennifer coming to him; he felt her arm come around his shoulder; but he couldn't think of her now. "Killed? She— Belinda was—" He wanted to throw up again. *Dear God.* All these years he'd blamed her, resented her, and she'd been—

"No, son, it wasn't deliberate," Fred hastened to say. "According to the letter it was a hit-and-run, an accidental death—which is still manslaughter if we find the man or woman who did it. They may show up at a police station one day and confess. Their conscience has been working, that's certain, or we wouldn't have got the letter telling us where your wife was buried."

"Buried?" Noah asked sharply.

Fred nodded. "She was found in the bushland southwest of Dural. She was wearing her wedding ring; dental records and DNA confirmed her identity. It's definitely your wife."

"Dural." The word came out dull, stupid. "You mean…"

"According to the dates given by the driver, she was killed the day she disappeared," Fred said gently. "She never ran off, but according to the letter, she was farther west of the shopping mall than we expected. It seems she must have gone for a long walk instead of shopping. She stepped out onto a crossing as the driver rounded a corner—a young person, we think, and probably speeding. Your wife didn't stand a chance." Fred shook his head. "It was a fairly isolated area, but still, how they got the bod—your wife in the car and took her away without anyone hearing anything, or seeing it happen, is beyond me. There'd be noise, and blood all over the road—"

"Fred," Jennifer interjected sharply.

Fred blinked, and the man re-emerged from the policeman. "I'm sorry, Noah," he said awkwardly. "Stupid thing to say."

Stupid? No, natural—Noah had thought the exact same thing. He guessed he'd never know how it was done, unless the person was caught.

Belinda hadn't left; a damned stupid speeding driver had torn his family apart…

It was curious, the way he felt—everything was spinning slowly around him, yet he was breathing hard and fast, as if he couldn't keep up. His mind felt blank and dizzy, yet the questions kept coming out of the darkness inside him. The only things touching him were the words Fred spoke, and the feel of Jennifer's arm, her fingers caressing his shoulder, like an anchor in sudden storm.

But counterbalancing that, there was only one reality, and the weight of it made it hard to breathe: *Belinda was guilty of nothing but a momentary lapse in judgment in leaving Cilla and Rowdy with a five-year-old Tim and a babysitter.*

For so long he'd almost hated her for leaving him, but she hadn't—she hadn't. Someone had taken her from them all.

"Why do you think the person confessed now?" Jennifer asked from behind him, and he was grateful for it; the darkness had turned blank with the thought. All these years, he'd blamed Belinda, and she was *dead.*

Fred shrugged. "Who knows? The people from the Missing Persons Unit think it might have been a show recently on a Sydney station, a documentary on the families of missing people, and how there's never any closure until the person, or their bodies, are found. If they saw that, perhaps your family in some way became real to them."

Noah nodded. That made sense, he supposed. He didn't know—he knew nothing at this point. "Thank you, Fred," he said, very politely. "Thank you for coming. If you'll excuse me now, I need to make some calls."

"The people from Missing Persons contacted your parents-in-law, and said there was news on your wife. They're on their way back with the kids. Did you want me here when you break it to them?"

Noah went cold all over, as if ice water had been tipped over him. He needed time to get his head together, and Peter and Jan would already be on the road. They took their damned caravan everywhere with them, like a stupid holy grail. It was always perfect, always ready to leave at a moment's notice, even with the kids there. They'd be only an hour or so from here by now. "No, thanks," he said quietly. "They'll want to contact the Missing Persons Unit themselves if they have questions or doubts." And they would. He knew that.

Not noticing his reaction, or tactfully overlooking it, Fred headed for the door. "Missing Persons said you know their number—they'll be here for a day or two if you or any member of your family has any questions for them." At the door, Fred turned back, twisting his hat in his hands before shoving it on his head. "I'm that sorry, Noah—for you, for the kids. I know you were hoping…" He turned to Jennifer, and nodded with obvious awkwardness. "Jennifer."

A hell of a strange situation for all of them, to say the least, but he couldn't hold onto the thought. Closure was finally here, just when he'd accepted it wouldn't come. And now he had to tell the kids, tell Peter and Jan—

The police car revved up, and the taillights disappeared up the driveway toward town.

Silence descended on the house—but it was a cheat. He had to get his head together, and fast, because the kids were on their way here, and he had to know what to say.

# CHAPTER TWELVE

"DO YOU want me to go?" Jennifer asked quietly after a few moments, feeling out of place here, with the man who'd proposed to her this day, the same day he found out his wife was dead.

Noah stared around at her, his eyes blank and unseeing. "No."

The word was plain, stark in its raw emotion. She shivered with the intensity of it. "Are you sure, Noah? Your parents-in-law will hate me being here."

There were many answers he could give to that, firstly that they weren't his parents-in-law anymore, and had no place in his private life. What she didn't expect was what he did say. "Don't go. I need you."

She shivered again, but came around the chair to face him, and slipped her hands into his. After a hesitation, she murmured, "How are you feeling?"

A moment passed, two…ten, twenty; then he finally said, "I don't know. I don't know."

His honesty hurt her. She knew she should be his friend now, to explore his feelings about Belinda since he'd discovered she'd never left him; but Jennifer couldn't make the words come. It was too much to ask of a woman in love.

Swallowing the hurting in her throat, blinking back the

tears of pain and half-shame, she tried to smile: a grim travesty of her glowing smiles today. "What do you need?"

He pulled his hands from hers, rubbing his forehead with the weary gesture that had touched her soul the day they'd met. "The right words to say to Tim, and to Peter and Jan."

Throwing up a brief, heartfelt prayer, she kept her distance: he didn't need a lover now. The right he'd given her today had vanished; she must accept that. She must let him go, give him the right to grieve. "There are no right words, Noah," she said gently. "You can't make this better for Tim."

He sighed and frowned—and she felt his withdrawal growing. She understood; she'd been there after Cody's death, sharing her deepest loss with no one.

To understand is to forgive, or so people said—but it didn't stop the heartache blossoming inside her like an evil vine. She moved back, physically and emotionally—slipping back to the role of friend she'd had only a few days ago, and accepted as right. "Would you like a coffee?"

He nodded, lost in his thoughts. "Thank you," he added vaguely.

When she put the mug in front of him, he didn't notice—and her nerves stretched to breaking point. What was she doing here? "You know what, the kids might need some comfort food when they get here. I think I'll just nick home and get the chocolate cake and cookies—"

*"No."*

It stopped her mid-stride; she turned back, half-inquiring, half-terrified. He was on his feet, staring wildly at her, half-seeing through a blur of tears, his arms wide-open and his face anguished. *"Jennifer."*

It was all she needed. She ran to him, throwing her arms around his neck. "I'm here, Noah," she whispered, holding him close, caressing his face, his shoulders and back.

"I can't feel anything," he whispered, shuddering. "I'm a widower about to bury my wife's remains and I can't even feel grief...I still *resent* her. She went for a walk, and was killed in a stupid accident. What right do I have to feel so much anger against her?"

Jennifer kissed his cheek, his lips: love without passion, giving all the love she had inside her. "I was angry with Cody, too. I wanted him to fight, to stay with me just one more day. But he looked up at me and whispered, 'I'm tired, Mummy'—and he stopped breathing soon after," she choked, feeling the grief swamp her over again in retelling it. "I almost *hated* him for that, a sick baby. He shouldn't have left me alone!"

Her outburst seemed to calm him. He wrapped his arms tight around her. "Not me—I'm angry for the sake of the kids," he rasped. "She shouldn't have gone for a walk without the kids, or gone shopping without me—we'd arranged that the last time I found out about her debts. She coped with depression by spending money we didn't have. She shouldn't have left the kids, even with the babysitter...but if she'd taken them..." He shuddered and buried his face in her throat. "I don't want to be angry with her, I don't want to hate her—but the last three years of hell wouldn't have happened if she'd kept her promise and waited for me!"

Finally she said it. "You're angry for—for still loving her so much when she's not here," she murmured, her heart breaking. He had the right to grieve, to love the wife who hadn't left him but *died*—but it didn't stop the pain; it made it worse.

"Love or anger, I don't know anymore. Everything's jumbled in my head. All I know is, I have to explain this to a little boy who's faithfully kept his promise to her for three years, and waited for her to keep hers and come home!"

"You'll find the words. You're his dad. He loves and trusts

you more than you know," she said, feeling helpless to say the right words.

"There's nothing to say. You know that. You said it yourself." He sighed against her throat. "What can you say when you have to shatter the dreams and hopes and faith of a little boy?"

The words, his warm breath, slid over her skin; his meaning touched her like a farewell.

Because it was. It was inevitable. There was too much between them, and yet not enough, not while he grieved and Tim would yet grieve; while she longed for the one thing she couldn't have, even while loving the daily reminder of Noah's love in the past.

Tim, Cilla, and Rowdy—she loved them so much; but she wasn't and never would be their mother. They were Belinda's children: Noah and Belinda's children. A fact as stark as her own: her tainted genetics would always create terminally ill children, and it would be too damn *painful* to raise Noah's kids. The first time she heard Tim say *you're not my mother,* it would break her.

She had to walk away. There was no option.

But when he lifted his face and closed his tear-wet eyes, seeking her mouth in near desperate hunger, she couldn't hold back. She knew this blind need, and let the kiss happen, allowed him to ravage her lips and crush her against him…and when his hands curved over her breasts, she moaned and arched into him. Celebrating life in the midst of grief and despair—oh, she knew that, too; but it didn't matter, nothing mattered but the overwhelming rush of love for him and his need for her colliding.

They fell back onto the sofa, kissing and touching. Wanting to forget all they had to face.

"I need you, Jennifer, I need you," he murmured as he

kissed her throat, rough and gravel-edged with desire and pain. "Don't go now, baby, don't…"

"Noah," she whispered back, turning her face to kiss his mouth again. Oh, the rush of beauty and wanting—it had never been like this for her before, and walking suddenly wasn't an option. "I'm here, Noah, I'm here."

"I thought I could take the risk—that I could be near you and walk away later, but I can't." He kissed her over and over, face, lips, throat and the hollow between her breasts; branding her as his with mouth and hands, caressing her in a fever that ignited hers, until her legs felt like jelly and her arms trembled with longing for more, for *everything*.

Longing to say the words that would change everything— then he nipped the corner between shoulder and throat as he caressed her breast, and words fled except one.

"Now," she whispered, arching up to him. "Now…"

He looked down at her, his eyes black and intense with desire. "The bedroom."

"Yes, yes." She got to her feet, then sat abruptly. "I don't think I can walk that far. I'm shaking," she confessed.

He smiled, his eyes softening in tenderness; then he swung her up in his arms, heading for his bedroom. "You're mine," he growled with soft nibbles to the vulnerable corner again, and she went limp in his arms. "I won't let you leave me, Jennifer. You hear me? *I won't let you leave.*"

Where had her gentle Noah gone? He sounded so fierce— and in those dark jeans and shirt he looked like a warrior fighting a battle in darkness. She shuddered in primitive response to it, unable to think beyond this moment; she loved him so *much*. She moaned, seeking his mouth again.

Lights on high beam turned into the driveway. The crunching of tyres over gravel came, and kept coming, as if a semi-trailer had turned in.

"The kids are here," she said, her voice flat and tight with thwarted passion.

Noah stilled, and looked down at her in tender command. "Tonight, Jennifer," he rasped as he slowly set her on her feet.

Sadness filled her; she shook her head. Their chance was gone.

He read her without any difficulty. His eyes burned into hers. "Tonight. There won't be regrets or second thoughts. You're mine."

She shuddered again, and clung to him until she was sure her legs would carry her weight. "I should go now."

"Don't go, Jennifer." He held up a hand as she tried to speak. "I know you're thinking of Peter and Jan and Tim—but Cilla and Rowdy will be confused and scared by all the emotion. They'll need someone...distanced from it. They'll need someone they love to explain it all to them. Maybe to take them out of it."

Jennifer gnawed on the inside of her lip, but there was no way to discount what he'd said. Cilla and Rowdy had no memories of Belinda, and the raw grief bound to come from Tim and their grandparents would confuse and frighten them.

"I'll stay," she said slowly, "until the children are asleep."

"And beyond," he added in quiet force. "Peter and Jan won't stay the night."

Before she could answer, the door flew open and Tim rushed in, his face alight and eager. "Dad! Dad, we're home. Nana and Pa said there's news of Mummy!"

In a moment, the sensual man became one hundred percent father. Noah watched his little boy running to him, knowing this would probably be the last time Tim *was* a little boy. He knelt down to catch his son in his arms. "Yes, matey," he said, gruff with sadness. "There's real news this time."

At Noah's tone of voice, Tim whitened and began to

struggle against him. "No…you're lying. Mummy just went away for a while!"

"Ah, matey." Noah held him gently. "They found her. Mummy never ran away, matey. She was hurt when she went out that day. She was gone all along. She's—at peace, Tim. She's not sad or hurting any more."

*"No. No!"*

The wail came from the open doorway, where Jan stood, clinging to the handle. She was white and shaking. "No…my girl, my Linnie…"

Tim slumped against Noah, with a high-pitched wail.

Peter was already dialling a number—the number for the Missing Persons Unit, no doubt.

Noah said quietly, "It's true, Peter. It was a hit-and-run. The driver finally got an attack of conscience and wrote a letter, telling where he'd buried her—and they found her."

And for some reason, the emotion overcame him. Three simple words changed his life. *They found her.* The choking ball of tightness cut off his breathing. One gulp, two—and the tears came at last, the tears he hadn't been able to shed since the day she'd gone missing. He held his little son in his arms and they cried together, while Peter yelled at the people from the Missing Persons Unit and Jan kept shaking her head, refusing to believe her daughter was—

But she knew it, just as Noah knew. Belinda was gone.

Peter was rapping out question after question to the person on the phone while Jan's face slowly crumpled, seeing the defeated slump to her husband's shoulders.

The dream was over. Though they'd refused to believe, Noah suspected they'd always known, deep down, because Belinda would never have left her family. She was dead, their daughter, his wife, the mother of his kids—and it was a damned stupid accident. Somebody in a rush to get somewhere, not thinking of the consequences—and a family had fallen apart...

*No, you didn't, Noah. You held them together. The kids are okay, thanks to you.*

In the midst of sudden, overwhelming grief, Belinda's voice came to him so clearly he almost turned around to find its source. Instead he wanted to thwack his head. He didn't *believe* in life after death, and—

*You chose well, Noah. She's a beautiful, loving woman. She'll be good to our kids.*

He couldn't help turning his head. She'd gathered Cilla and Rowdy onto her lap on the sofa in the furthest corner of the room, holding them close as Cilla sucked her thumb furiously and Rowdy, frightened by all the grief, was crying too. Jennifer's face was filled with tenderness as she held them and told them she was here, that it was all right to cry.

Cilla laid her head on Jennifer's breast and escaped the only way she could, falling asleep; and Jennifer held her and caressed her hair, while murmuring loving words to Rowdy, whose tears were already subsiding.

Tim kept beating his fists against Noah's chest, with those sad little wails, slowly descending to hiccups. Noah murmured over and over, "It's all right, matey. She never left you. She loved you—she loved us all. It wasn't her fault—she never left you."

Peter finally hung up the phone and just stared at his wife, his eyes filled with horror and devastation. Jan collapsed on Peter, sobbing.

Tim hiccupped and looked up at Noah. "Nana and Pa said..."

Noah knew what Tim couldn't say. "They needed to believe it was my fault, Tim. I always understood that." He looked up briefly at his mother-in-law. "They needed to believe she was alive. They wanted a reason for her not wanting to come home."

His son nodded. "But…it wasn't your fault," he whispered. "Dad…"

The tears streaking down his face blended with Tim's as he felt him close again. "Ah, don't, matey. I know. You had to keep your promise."

Tim sobbed against his chest, whispering, *"Daddy, Daddy."*

And finally, after three long years, Noah knew his little son would be all right. He'd come home at last. In being found, Belinda had released Tim from the promise that had become an unbearable burden for eight-year-old shoulders.

*Closure.* It was as if Belinda had somehow given them all her blessing in moving on, in finding healing…

"What is *she* doing here?"

Jan's accusing voice startled them all. Cilla jumped in Jennifer's lap, and started crying; Rowdy wailed again—and Tim noticed Jennifer for the first time. "Jen…my mummy's dead," he sobbed, and ran to her. Somehow Jennifer found a few inches more space on her lap for him, crooning soft words of comfort.

Peter and Jan gasped, as if Tim had betrayed them. Noah groaned inside. They needed to be angry right now, and they'd found the perfect target.

"What is *she* doing here?" Jan snapped. "She's an outsider. She didn't know Linnie!"

But Noah had had enough. "Stop right there, Jan. Jennifer's a close family friend, she minds Cilla and Rowdy most days, and the kids love her."

"She's an outsider. She doesn't deserve to be here!" Peter yelled.

*"She didn't know Linnie!"* Jan near-screamed, setting off all three kids into terrified tears.

"No, she didn't, but she knows the kids—and for once in three years, I'd like you to put your grandchildren's welfare before your feelings. Tonight isn't about Belinda. This is about my kids' needs—and they need Jennifer!"

"Get out. Get out!" Jan screamed at Jennifer—but Noah stepped into her range of sight.

"This is my home, Jan. I've told you Jennifer's welcome," he said coldly. "I loved Belinda all my life, too. I know you're grieving, but I will not allow you to take it out on Jennifer. Belinda's gone, and the kids love and need Jennifer—and so do I."

Jan gasped and whitened. Peter stepped forward with clenched fists. "Damn you, boy, you only just found out our girl—*your wife*—is gone!" he yelled.

Noah held up a hand. "How many more years do I have to live alone to prove to you that I loved her?" he asked wearily. "You've set Tim up as my watchdog, stopping any-one from getting near. You've reminded him of his promise over and over, keeping the family ready for Belinda's return. You now know it's not going to happen. And despite his best efforts, Tim loves Jennifer as much as Cilla and Rowdy—"

"His real name is Jesse," Peter snarled. "Linnie named him Jesse!"

"—and I'm not going to allow you to damage that for your need to keep Belinda alive. My kids will always know who their mother was—I'll make sure of that. But she's gone, and these kids need a mother. And I need Jennifer. I love her, and I want to marry her."

Jan burst into tears again. Peter stood over Noah, his face mottled with fury…but Noah's focus was on the silent woman holding his kids. What she was thinking about his declaration.

"You forget quickly," Peter sneered. "It shows what my girl meant to you."

"Enough," he snarled, so harshly Peter took a step back. "I

won't apologise for putting a new life together for myself and the kids. We've been through enough pain."

He met his father-in-law's eyes without flinching. "I've only got one more thing to say. For three years I've allowed you to blame me for everything. But you've damaged Tim—and I won't allow that anymore. I wasn't responsible for Belinda's disappearance—you know that now. You'll always be welcome here, and be a part of the kids' lives—but I'll never let you hurt them this way again. Belinda would never have allowed it."

At the mention of her name, both their faces crumpled, and he knew it had been a low, if necessary blow. This was the first day of their grief—until now they'd lived in fear and determination, but never allowed grief to be part of their emotions.

"I'm sorry," he said quietly, "but it had to be said. You both need time now to grieve—but the kids and I need to move on. We've done our share."

"I want to go see the Missing Persons people." Peter turned his back on Noah. "The kids' bags will be on the verandah." He held out his arms to the kids. "Nana and Pa have to go now. Be good for—for Daddy," he said, his voice gruff with tears, "and don't you ever forget your mummy."

He glared at Jennifer when the kids hesitated.

"Go to Pa," she said softly, avoiding Noah's eyes. "Kiss Nana and Pa goodbye, and thank them for your lovely holiday."

As the kids hugged Jan and Peter, Noah thought of the holiday the kids hadn't had, and vowed to take them back to the Gold Coast as soon as the weather grew warmer.

Then he noticed Jennifer, sitting stiff and still on the sofa. She wasn't looking at him—she hadn't looked at him since he'd stated his intentions to Jan and Peter.

She didn't look like a woman in love. She looked as if she desperately wanted to bolt.

# CHAPTER THIRTEEN

IT WAS after ten by the time they finally got the kids to bed. She'd sung a dozen lullabies to Cilla, and they'd had to lay on either side of Tim and hold him as he cried himself to sleep.

Rowdy, tired out by his crying, had fallen asleep hours ago, even before dinner.

In the living room again, Jennifer stretched, feeling the bones crack in her back. She was so tired—but there was more to come. There was no way Noah would let her leave without...

The gulp hurt her throat and chest. He had the right to expect *something* from her. If she'd meant her rejection today, she shouldn't have kissed him and allowed him to touch her with such intimacy. She shouldn't have almost demanded they make love.

And oh, how she still wanted to—she ached for him—but could she take him into her arms, spend the night in his bed, and then reject his proposal a second time?

When she heard his step on the floorboards, she almost turned tail and ran. Then she felt ashamed. If Noah could face her the day his proposal was rejected, he discovered he was a widower, confronted his parents-in-law and brought his son to terms with the loss of his mother, what right did she have to be a coward?

So she swung around and smiled at him. "Quite a day, huh?"

He didn't bother with preliminaries. His red-rimmed eyes bored into hers, no compromise, no surrender. "But it's over for us, isn't it? Just tell me the truth, Jennifer. I'm too bloody tired to tap-dance around it."

It seemed this was the week her gentle Noah came into his own. He wasn't going to stop her—but he wouldn't let her off the hook, either. If she was going, she had to do so honestly. She walked over to him, lifted her hands and, seeing the flat distance in his eyes, let them fall. "A lot of things have changed since this afternoon," she said, feeling her way.

"But not your decision, right?" he asked, sounding unutterably weary. "You haven't looked at me since I told my in-laws I wanted to marry you."

She spread her hands wide, praying he'd understand. "I told you why I wouldn't remarry. That hasn't changed. It never will."

"You're turning me down because you want my baby. You love me the way I love you, but you can't have my baby, so all five of us have to suffer the consequences. You don't get one thing you want, so we all miss out on happiness. Is that it?"

The casual-seeming words made her catch her breath, then it got stuck there, choking her. She coughed and coughed, but it did nothing; the stinging came, the tears welled up, filling her eyes. "Noah…"

"Is that everything?" His tone was almost conversational. "You were the one who said we can't always get what we want. So I lose the love of the rest of my life for a genetic defect, and my kids lose the mother they adore because they're not enough for you."

She did gasp then. "It's not that!" It was the other way around…wasn't it? That she wasn't enough for them?

He went on as if she hadn't spoken. "Yeah, it looks like we don't always get what we want—but walking away from me, from us, still isn't going to give you a baby. Nothing's going to do that—but for some reason, you think punishing us all for your broken dreams will work for you."

"No!" It was a strangled croak now. "I never said that, or thought it…Noah, please…"

"Didn't you? Didn't you say that?" Suddenly he was right in her face, speaking with guttural demand. "Because that's what I could have sworn you said. You love me, but I'm not enough. You want my baby, but the three kids I have, all little more than babies, aren't enough, either. They have to have your genetic code, or have come from your body, to be worth a lifetime of love."

The bald fury of his statement knocked her arguments down flat. "It…it's not that…"

"Isn't it?"

A lifetime of longing, of knowledge of what she'd always dreamed of having, withered and died before the raw pain in his eyes. She didn't know what to say. Nothing would make this right. How could she say it? *Tell me it's real—tell me you love me as much as you love Belinda. Tell me the grief I saw tonight wasn't the raw grief of a man still in love with his wife!*

Second best, always second best in her life. A life where she either replaced what she wanted with next best, or she *was* next best. She could never be the woman he'd loved since he was thirteen, but she could be a great wife and mother…a terrific *replacement.*

She couldn't do it. One of them she could handle, but both would break her in two.

"I'm sorry," she faltered, feeling more inadequate, more foolish than she ever had in her life. "There couldn't be a worse day for this…"

"There is no right day, Jennifer." He turned away, his body stiff, his face white. "I have to pull a miracle out of a hat to be good enough for you. The fact that you're leaving me the day I find out my wife's dead is beside the point. My falling in love with you was my decision, my problem. I'm a man and can handle losing you if I have to. But the fact that you made my kids love and rely on you—to look on you as a mother, when you never meant to stay—that I couldn't believe of you."

She stepped back, almost falling over, but found nothing to say. *Do you? Do you love me, Noah, now you know Belinda never left you, but died?* It rang in her mind, but somehow it seemed ridiculously selfish, given all he and his family had been through today.

He wouldn't even look at her now. "Did you ever think of what you were doing, Jennifer, in making three motherless kids love and depend on you? If you never intended to give us a chance, why didn't you keep a professional distance with them, like you do with the other kids?"

Her mind totally spaced on that. Suddenly it wasn't about her, but the kids—if she'd hurt them… "I…I didn't mean to…to—I thought…"

"What?"

"They—needed me more than the other kids," she faltered. "I just wanted to help. I thought of myself as a transitional mother—someone to help them heal. Then when you found them another mother, they'd be ready…"

"Very noble of you," he mocked quietly. "No, I'm sure you even believed it, for a while. But you must have seen how dependent they were becoming? You knew I wasn't playing games, either. I'm not that kind of man. So at what point did you start blinding yourself to the damage you could do to them, because you loved playing house with us? When did we become your disposable family? Did you set a date for when it would end, or was there a plan to introduce me to the kids' new mother at the right place and time?"

It was as if he was holding a mirror up to her face, and she could see herself clearly for the first time since Cody's death. She'd indulged in playing house with the Brannigans, without thinking of the long-term consequences to those adorable, motherless children—or to a man who had struggled for years on his own.

All she'd wanted to do was help, to be close to them; but without meaning it, she'd played God with the Brannigan family, and it was they who would pay the price.

"Don't come back here, Jennifer. Don't come near me, or my kids, unless you intend to stay for life. Don't play house with us anymore. My kids aren't your dollies."

She'd never heard him so harsh, or inflexible. He meant every word. There'd be no more midnight kisses in her kitchen or on blankets; no more smiles, no hugs or childish chatter to fill her life. *No Noah.* No more words of love, whether she was the love of his life or second best.

It was over. She didn't deserve them.

With a tiny cry she turned and bolted out the door, and even made it to the back field before she started throwing up.

*Six weeks later*

"Dad, that's hot. You need the oven mitt." Tim raced over from the table to give Noah the protective cover.

"Thanks, mate," Noah said, realising what he'd been about to do. He put on the mitt before getting dinner out of the oven. He served up the food for them, and sat at the table, correcting the kids when they needed it, cutting up Rowdy and Cilla's food—but he didn't eat himself. The kind of kiddie food they liked best had lost its appeal six weeks ago.

He felt Tim watching him, with the same anxiety he'd been watching the past two weeks since coming back home from

Sydney, where they'd had the funeral for Belinda. "Tim, you're not eating enough, matey," he said, to distract him.

"You aren't eating at all."

The aggressive tone startled him; Tim had been so quiet since they came home. Noah frowned and looked down at the food and pushed it away. "Just not hungry tonight, I guess."

"You haven't been hungry since we got home," Tim shouted. "You've been all weird for weeks, since you stopped being friends with Jen. If you want her back so bad, why don't you just go and get her?"

Rowdy burst into tears. Cilla sucked hard on her thumb... and they all looked at him like they expected him to make their lives right.

He was failing them all over again. Nothing was damned *right* since Jennifer refused him. His family was falling apart again...

Noah felt the blood drain from his face. "Stop it, Tim," he said, very quietly. "Stop it."

And he pushed back his chair and went outside to run again, up and down the field. He didn't leave them alone, but stayed where they could yell for him, but he ran and ran, and ran...

Five minutes later, Tim climbed out his bedroom window.

Noah was running again.

Jennifer closed her eyes. She had to stop watching the Brannigan house from the window, or she'd go insane...

But moments later, she was looking again. What else did she have to do?

It was only now that, when it was too late to change things, she knew how *empty* her life was without them. She'd gone back to quilting circle, took on more kids, went to church and the fundraising sessions and town improvement meetings, but none of it helped the tightness in her chest and the feeling that she wanted to be sick all the time. Veronica and Jessie had stopped making jokes about the sexy man next door weeks ago. They didn't mention him at all after the first night, when they'd seen her reaction.

There was nothing to say, nothing could help, and the ache in her heart just grew and grew, because unlike Cody, the people she loved were alive. She could be with them all now, if she hadn't been so blind and so stupid.

*So go to him, go to them.*

And say what? *I'm the world's prize idiot, I don't deserve any of you but I need and love you and please, please accept second best?*

Suddenly she squinted, concentrating. Yes, even from this distance, in the light of a strong full moon, she could see the small figure climbing out his window…

Jennifer closed her eyes, throwing up a brief prayer for him to come to her, and not to run away again.

It seemed she was answered. He came straight to the boundary fence and hopped over it, and ran to the verandah. "Jen! Jen," he whispered urgently. "Jen!"

She was at the door before the last call. Seeing the blazing intensity of his eyes—Noah's eyes—she gathered him into her arms. "Tim, what is it, sweetie?" She drew him inside the house. "Would you like a cookie?"

Tim shook his head, his gaze fixed on her. "Why aren't you our friend anymore?" he asked so bluntly Jennifer caught her breath. "Don't you love…um, Cilla and Rowdy anymore?"

Even amid a pain so strong it clawed at her heart, she wanted to smile; but she kept a straight face and said, "Of course I do, Tim—I love you all."

"Then why don't Cilla and Rowdy stay with you anymore? Why did Dad get someone else to finish the verandah and cubby house while we were gone? Why are you selling the house and going away? Why don't we have dinner here and play now? We—Cilla and Rowdy, I mean—miss it here! They miss you!"

The words were fierce with the pain he was trying so hard to hide—and her heart melted. "If your dad will let you come, Tim, you are always welcome here. Always."

But he didn't let her off the hook. "Why does Dad get so—so *sad* and white when we want to see you? He—he's as sad as Mummy used to be." The glitter in his eyes became full-blown tears and his mouth trembled. "I'm *scared,* Jen!" he wailed. "Daddy's not the same, and I can't make him better. He doesn't eat much and he just runs and runs and is sad all the time!"

Jennifer held him close, rocking him. "Oh, baby. Oh, Tim. I'm so sorry." She hesitated. "Is Daddy really so sad?" The boy nodded, his head against her breast, and she ached with sweetness—she loved this strong, vulnerable boy so much! "Do you think he's sad because of your mummy?"

Tim wrenched himself out of her arms. "No. I *know* it's 'cause he misses you. He won't even *look* over here. Cilla and Rowdy miss you. *Why* don't you come over, Jen?"

There was no way to avoid it; she must be honest. "Your dad wants to marry me, Tim, but I—I thought I couldn't do that."

"Why? Is—is it 'cause of me? 'Cause I've been so naughty?" Pleading eyes turned to her. "I can be good, Jen. I—I promise I'll be good."

"Oh, Tim!" She wrapped him close in her arms, kissing his forehead, his cheeks. "You *are* a good boy. It wasn't that—"

Tim's voice came out all muffled when he finally spoke. "I'm not a little kid anymore, Jen. I know you love Dad, 'cause you always look at him all goofy." Jennifer had to choke back the laughter and tears at once. "Why won't you be our mummy?" he cried again.

She hesitated. "It wasn't you, or your family. It's—it's me. I have a problem…"

"Can't you make it go away?" His voice was half-muffled in her shoulder.

"No," she said, sadness touching her soul at speaking of Cody, but with Tim in her arms, it didn't have that exquisite agony. "I—I lost my little boy a few years ago, you see. Cody died, like your mummy died. He was very sick. I have something wrong with me, you see. If I have more babies they could be sick, too. And—and that made me sad. I thought I'd miss it too much." *But not as much as I've missed all of you,* she suddenly thought.

Tim pulled back to look at her, his eyes desperate. "But that's not fair! Can't—can't Rowdy be like your little boy? Can't he hug you and—and be like him? And Cilla could be your little girl? We *need* a mummy, Jen!" he cried, trembling all over with emotion. "Dad doesn't smile anymore, and—and Cilla's sucking her thumb all the time and climbin' trees again, and Rowdy just *cries.* He doesn't even wanna play anymore…" His tears spilled, and he dashed at them with a fist. "They *need* you, Jen. Please, won't you be our—I mean, their mummy? And be nice to Daddy again, and make him happy? If—if you want more hugs, I'd even give you some," he finished, his face filled with brave determination. "If you want *two* little boys, I can be your little boy, too."

Oh, the courage of this magnificent, hurting child! Out of the mouths of babes came truth—a truth that did indeed set her free.

She might never have the baby her heart craved, but if there was something the past six weeks had taught her, it was that life with the Brannigans held a joy that stopped it ever being second-best. She missed the hugs and kisses from the children, so much more so than any of the children she minded—

And it wasn't because they needed her: she needed them. From the first day, her heart had known what her stubborn mind refused to see. She'd loved them like a mother all along…and she loved Noah, loved him so much she felt dead inside without him.

She had two choices: she could have almost everything she'd ever wanted, or nothing at all—and nothing meant emptiness and regret for life. Almost everything was far better than second best. Just having Tim with her now, she *felt* like a mother. She felt *loved.*

"So you think your dad's missing me, sweetheart?" she asked softly, her heart racing. *With joy.* She was going home, home to her babies, to her beautiful Noah…

"I know he does. He gets so sad when we want to see you, and—" Tim's face lit up. "Jen?" he whispered, trembling with excitement.

Jen nodded, smiled and kissed him. "Tim, you are the best boy in the whole world, and I would be so proud to have you for one of my boys—but never a *little* boy. That can be Rowdy's job." She laughed at the relief lighting up his expressive eyes. "Can you climb back through that window, and do exactly what I ask you to do?"

# CHAPTER FOURTEEN

THE fire had gone out again.

With a savage sound of impatience, Noah got out the box of fire-lighters again, and, giving up on economy, put four cubes under the logs at once, screwed up newspaper as well and put it everywhere, and lit it all. He stepped back, locked the fire guards into place and stood there watching, hands shoved in pockets and kicking at a piece of coal.

How could a life so full, with so little free time, still feel so empty?

Tim's words had been bashing around in his head like a hollow drum for the past hour or more. *If you want Jen back so bad, why don't you go and get her?*

Six weeks—such a short time, yet it felt like a year since he'd seen her.

He didn't look up the hill. He *didn't* look for her lights at night, and wonder if she'd come to him. It was obvious she was avoiding him. He knew better than to look. She hadn't changed her mind. She loved him, but not enough.

He might have looked for her during the first few days after they'd come back from the funeral, but not now.

*What funeral?* He thought grimly. What he'd done was formally identify his wife from her wedding-ring and rotten wallet, and arranged a travesty of a service because the police wouldn't release the remains for burial. She was still *an open case,* because of the letter…but the kids didn't need to know that.

Now Peter and Jan had begun a new crusade: finding Belinda's accidental killer. He didn't blame them for it. Parents always wanted justice and right for their children, and Peter and Jan's whole life had revolved around their daughter. He had more immediate priorities: his kids. He wasn't going to let his former parents-in-law damage the kids by talking of justice, or say their Mummy wasn't at peace yet, and why.

There were times when the fight just wasn't worth the cost.

He felt that Belinda was finally at peace with the finding of her body—but he wasn't. He'd said he could handle losing Jennifer—but all the way through the ordeal of looking at the wedding ring, the rotten wallet and the skeletal remains, and through a sham service with an empty coffin, a wailing son and dry-eyed, vengeful parents-in-law, all he could think was *why, Jennifer? Why the hell didn't you love me enough to be with me now?*

He'd thought he was strong enough. He'd lost the love of his young life and survived, and brought up his kids the best he could…but the pain of losing Jennifer was getting worse every damned day. He'd done all he could. He'd fought for her, he'd—

*Hadn't he?*

He blinked, and again. Had he fought, truly fought for Jennifer?

He hadn't been passive; he'd fought to make her love him—but had he left something, anything undone?

The past three or four years had taught him to put the kids above his own needs—they must come first. In submerging everything that made him a man for too long, he'd buried his wants, his desires—his *love*—for the sake of Tim's fears…

Even when he'd met Jennifer, and knew she loved him,

when she'd made her decision to walk away, he'd let her do it. He'd let her go rather than risk it all, instead of truly fighting for her, because *the kids* would be hurt—

*Rubbish. They were your excuse and you know it. You were too scared to be a man again...*

*If you want her so bad, go and get her!*

With that the man in him roared to life—the man he'd lost to the father three years ago—and he would no longer be denied. What was he doing here alone, when the love of his life was five hundred feet away, loving him as he loved her?

Before he thought it through, he stalked through the door toward Jennifer's house. He'd do whatever it took to make her say yes. Failure wasn't an option.

"Dad!" called an imperative voice from the house. "Dad!"

Noah turned, but only for a moment. "No, Tim. Go back to bed. You're fine, and the kids are safe. I'll be back in fifteen minutes. I've got my phone if you need me."

"But I've got a surprise, Dad—it will make you happy—"

"It can wait," he shouted back, resuming his relentless stride.

"Where are you going, Dad?" Tim yelled, sounding frantic.

"To get Jennifer!" He didn't care at this point if Tim rebelled; his son *needed* Jennifer, even if he didn't know it yet.

But after a moment, a cry of "Waahoo!" came from the house. "Go, Dad, go get her!"

Despite his grim determination, a smile curved his mouth.

Lights were on in her house, but he didn't care if he woke her, or knocked the door down. If she was anything like him, she wasn't sleeping anyway. He hopped the boundary fence—

"Jennifer!" he roared as he strode up the stairs to the back door of the house he'd known as home from the first day. The *woman* he'd known was his the first day. "Jennifer!" He pounded on the door.

Moments later the door swung open, and a breathless

woman in the throes of putting on lipstick and combing her hair at once, by the look of the things in her hand, gazed at him. The smile wavered on her lips, fear and joy at once, her whole face filled with love…*with love.* "Noah," she whispered, her eyes drinking him in with wide-eyed wonder and joy, like she was a kid having her first glimpse at Disneyland.

Without a word he scooped her against him and kissed her, deep, drugging kisses filled with demand. "You're mine," he growled between kisses. He moulded her body to his, curving his hand around her waist and hip until she moaned, dropped lipstick and hair comb, completely melted against him and kissed him back with the same insatiable hunger he felt. "I *love* you, and you love me and you're going to marry me. I won't give you up for a dream you can't even have. I won't give you up because you think you're not enough for us. You are—you *love* my kids and they love you, and it's more than enough. We belong together—you, me, the kids—all of us. I'm not asking you to marry me—I'm *telling* you."

She pulled back, her eyes shining. "Yes, Noah," she said softly. "Yes."

He made another growling sound and kissed her again. "You'd better mean it, because I'm taking it as a promise. We're getting the rings tomorrow, and I'm calling my parents to fly home. We'll need them to mind the kids while we're on our honeymoon."

Jennifer gave a low, throaty laugh that made his body tighten even more. "Yes, darling," she murmured with a teasing wink. "And are you going to tell me when the wedding is and where? My brother and sisters and their families might want to come to my wedding, and my parents will need to fly home, too."

He grinned and kissed her again, deep and hot, until they forgot the questions for a while. "Thirty-four days," he whispered against her mouth. "We get the licence tomorrow, and marry the day we legally can. And—" thinking on his feet had worked quite well in the past half hour "—how does the Barrier Reef sound for a honeymoon? We could get my parents to mind the kids on a family-friendly resort, and we could sail around the islands. We could visit them every few days, and be close enough for contact..."

"And still have time alone," she whispered, her eyes shining. "I can't wait." Her kiss was deep, with an urgency that told him the past weeks had been as hard for her as for him. "I love you so much, Noah. I've missed you like crazy."

"I can tell." He grinned down at her, but with a strange feeling inside. He supposed simple family happiness was something he'd have to get used to again—but he didn't think it would be very hard. Not with Jennifer as his wife.

She laughed again, and buffed him lightly on the chin. "Let's go tell the kids."

"I thought you'd make it harder for me than this," he said after the next kiss, as he turned her around, heading for his house.

"You underrate yourself," she said quietly. "There hasn't been a day, an hour, when I haven't wanted to turn the clock back and say yes, or run over to you. I've missed you so much."

He helped her over the fence, not because she needed it, but he wouldn't let go of her for a moment. "You could have come to me." But right now, the past didn't matter; she was where he needed her to be—with him, loving him. It was enough. More than enough.

"I couldn't. I didn't know if you loved me, Noah—not after you knew Belinda didn't leave you," she said quietly. "You said the words, but I didn't *feel* them. Probably because I didn't believe I was worthy of you. I thought—if you missed me enough, if you loved me enough, you'd come to me. And you did..."

He stopped, turned her in his arms and cupped her face in his hands. "Jennifer," he whispered. "Jennifer." The long, tender kiss showed her without words just what she meant to him. "Even if she'd been alive, I couldn't have gone back. I'm not the boy she married anymore—and the man I've become is yours. I knew it even as Fred told me she was gone. I thought you knew it, too."

She shook her head. "That night…what you said. I felt so ashamed, Noah." Her voice quivered with shame through the happiness. "I was selfish, punishing all of us for a dream I can't do anything to change. I didn't feel like I deserved you all."

He nuzzled her throat. "I'll remind you of that every time we fight, or the kids play up," he said, his voice filled with sudden laughter, and she wrapped herself around him, chuckling and kissing him. "But you said 'didn't' deserve me. Seriously, what changed your mind?"

"Not what—who," she murmured through kisses to his throat, making him groan with pleasures to come. "You should be very proud of your oldest son. He proposed to me on your behalf thirty minutes ago—for your sake, and for Cilla and Rowdy. He was worried about you all, and I knew that in punishing myself, I was only hurting us all. He showed me that I *am* their mother already, whether I deserved it or not. He also told me how much you were missing me," she added with an impish note in her voice. "I'll remind you of *that* every time we fight."

He grinned again. "So that was Tim's surprise just now? You were coming to me?"

"Yup. You've raised an amazing boy, Mr. Brannigan."

"He's got a lot of raising time yet, Mrs. Brannigan-to-be," he said, just to hear the sound of it. "Jennifer Brannigan."

"Jennifer Louisa Millicent Brannigan." She rolled her eyes. "What a mouthful…but it'll be worth it, to have you."

And they stopped for another kiss, the passion leaving them breathless and aching.

The door opened before they could knock. Joyful screams came the moment the light from inside the house spilled over them. A pyjama-clad Cilla and Rowdy, tousled, bright-eyed and eager, jumped into Jennifer's arms, squealing and asking when they could call her Mummy and when they were coming back to her place every day.

Jennifer staggered back a little under the combined weight of the kids, her eyes alight with joy. "Right now for both, if you want to," she replied, winking at Tim, blowing a kiss in his direction. "Tim, being a big boy, might want to keep calling me Jen?" She turned to the little kids, hugging and kissing them, telling them how *much* she'd missed them…leaving Tim to make his own decision, in his way and time.

Noah swallowed a lump in his throat at her understanding, loving Tim just as he was without trying to change him. How did he ever get so lucky?

"I woke the kids to tell them," Tim told Noah importantly, with a massive grin. A grin still touched with sorrow—he had some healing yet to do. But after his unselfish act tonight, Noah had no doubt his son would make it—that they'd all make it now. With Jennifer by his side, his family would be just fine…and he'd be the happiest man alive.

The first miracle at the March house had been the woman who lived inside it—and the second, that she'd needed them as much as they needed her; that she loved him as he loved her. He didn't need to ask for a third miracle: he knew they'd love each other, be a family for life.

Jennifer smiled at him, as if knowing what he was thinking, and announced, "It's celebration time—and I have loads of ice cream and cookies in my freezer! We're going to have a late-night snack, just for the fun of it. Go sit at the table, and

Dad and I will be there in a minute. Tim, can you get the stuff
out for me?"

"Sure, Jen," Tim grinned. "Let's go, kids!"

Cilla and Rowdy hurrahed, and then bolted after Tim
toward Jennifer's house, leaving them alone.

A pair of warm, loving arms slipped around his waist.
Noah turned in her arms, smiling down into her glowing face.
"What is it?" he asked, seeing she needed to say something.

She hugged him, but bit her lip. "I adore the kids—you
know that—but I'm not marrying you for them. You know
that, don't you?" Her gaze on his was a touch anxious.

He grinned. "With the way you look at me, and touch me?
I know you're marrying me for my body." And he laughed as
she swatted him.

"The worst thing is you're partly right. I can hardly wait
to get you naked," she murmured in his ear, sending shudders
of need, of desire, all the way through him. "I'm going to be
a demanding wife, love."

"The kids are waiting for ice cream and you say that to me?
You're killing me, woman," he groaned.

"I'll make it up to you." Her eyes shone with promise. "Just
as soon as we're alone…"

"Dad! Jen! Ice cream! Cookies, Mummy!"

The cries from three young throats broke the frantic kiss.
They leaned on each other's foreheads, smiling, knowing this
was life as it was meant to be. Then she whispered, "Race
you!" and they headed for the house, toward kids and cookies
and ice cream and love.

For home.

1007 Gen Std HB

# NOVEMBER 2007 HARDBACK TITLES

## ROMANCE

| | |
|---|---|
| **The Italian Billionaire's Ruthless Revenge** *Jacqueline Baird* | 978 0 263 19716 7 |
| **Accidentally Pregnant, Conveniently Wed** *Sharon Kendrick* | 978 0 263 19717 4 |
| **The Sheikh's Chosen Queen** *Jane Porter* | 978 0 263 19718 1 |
| **The Frenchman's Marriage Demand** *Chantelle Shaw* | 978 0 263 19719 8 |
| **The Millionaire's Convenient Bride** *Catherine George* | 978 0 263 19720 4 |
| **Expecting His Love-Child** *Carol Marinelli* | 978 0 263 19721 1 |
| **The Greek Tycoon's Unexpected Wife** *Annie West* | 978 0 263 19722 8 |
| **The Italian's Captive Virgin** *India Grey* | 978 0 263 19723 5 |
| **Her Hand in Marriage** *Jessica Steele* | 978 0 263 19724 2 |
| **The Sheikh's Unsuitable Bride** *Liz Fielding* | 978 0 263 19725 9 |
| **The Bridesmaid's Best Man** *Barbara Hannay* | 978 0 263 19726 6 |
| **A Mother in a Million** *Melissa James* | 978 0 263 19727 3 |
| **The Rancher's Doorstep Baby** *Patricia Thayer* | 978 0 263 19728 0 |
| **Moonlight and Roses** *Jackie Braun* | 978 0 263 19729 7 |
| **Their Miracle Child** *Gill Sanderson* | 978 0 263 19730 3 |
| **Single Dad, Nurse Bride** *Lynne Marshall* | 978 0 263 19731 0 |

## HISTORICAL

| | |
|---|---|
| **The Vanishing Viscountess** *Diane Gaston* | 978 0 263 19778 5 |
| **A Wicked Liaison** *Christine Merrill* | 978 0 263 19779 2 |
| **Virgin Slave, Barbarian King** *Louise Allen* | 978 0 263 19780 8 |

## MEDICAL™

| | |
|---|---|
| **The Italian's New-Year Marriage Wish** *Sarah Morgan* | 978 0 263 19824 9 |
| **The Doctor's Longed-For Family** *Joanna Neil* | 978 0 263 19825 6 |
| **Their Special-Care Baby** *Fiona McArthur* | 978 0 263 19826 3 |
| **A Family for the Children's Doctor** *Dianne Drake* | 978 0 263 19827 0 |

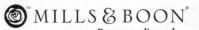 **MILLS & BOON**
*Pure reading pleasure*

1007 Gen Std LP

# NOVEMBER 2007 LARGE PRINT TITLES

## ROMANCE

| | |
|---|---|
| **Bought: The Greek's Bride** *Lucy Monroe* | 978 0 263 19495 1 |
| **The Spaniard's Blackmailed Bride** *Trish Morey* | 978 0 263 19496 8 |
| **Claiming His Pregnant Wife** *Kim Lawrence* | 978 0 263 19497 5 |
| **Contracted: A Wife for the Bedroom** *Carol Marinelli* | 978 0 263 19498 2 |
| **The Forbidden Brother** *Barbara McMahon* | 978 0 263 19499 9 |
| **The Lazaridis Marriage** *Rebecca Winters* | 978 0 263 19500 2 |
| **Bride of the Emerald Isle** *Trish Wylie* | 978 0 263 19501 9 |
| **Her Outback Knight** *Melissa James* | 978 0 263 19502 6 |

## HISTORICAL

| | |
|---|---|
| **Dishonour and Desire** *Juliet Landon* | 978 0 263 19409 8 |
| **An Unladylike Offer** *Christine Merrill* | 978 0 263 19410 4 |
| **The Roman's Virgin Mistress** *Michelle Styles* | 978 0 263 19411 1 |

## MEDICAL™

| | |
|---|---|
| **A Bride for Glenmore** *Sarah Morgan* | 978 0 263 19371 8 |
| **A Marriage Meant To Be** *Josie Metcalfe* | 978 0 263 19372 5 |
| **Dr Constantine's Bride** *Jennifer Taylor* | 978 0 263 19373 2 |
| **His Runaway Nurse** *Meredith Webber* | 978 0 263 19374 9 |
| **The Rescue Doctor's Baby Miracle** *Dianne Drake* | 978 0 263 19547 7 |
| **Emergency at Riverside Hospital** *Joanna Neil* | 978 0 263 19548 4 |

**MILLS & BOON**
*Pure reading pleasure*

# DECEMBER 2007 HARDBACK TITLES

## ROMANCE

| | |
|---|---|
| **The Greek Tycoon's Defiant Bride** *Lynne Graham* | 978 0 263 19732 7 |
| **The Italian's Rags-to-Riches Wife** *Julia James* | 978 0 263 19733 4 |
| **Taken by Her Greek Boss** *Cathy Williams* | 978 0 263 19734 1 |
| **Bedded for the Italian's Pleasure** *Anne Mather* | 978 0 263 19735 8 |
| **The Sheikh's Virgin Princess** *Sarah Morgan* | 978 0 263 19736 5 |
| **The Virgin's Wedding Night** *Sara Craven* | 978 0 263 19737 2 |
| **Innocent Wife, Baby of Shame** *Melanie Milburne* | 978 0 263 19738 9 |
| **The Sicilian's Ruthless Marriage Revenge** *Carole Mortimer* | 978 0 263 19739 6 |
| **Cattle Rancher, Secret Son** *Margaret Way* | 978 0 263 19740 2 |
| **Rescued by the Sheikh** *Barbara McMahon* | 978 0 263 19741 9 |
| **Her One and Only Valentine** *Trish Wylie* | 978 0 263 19742 6 |
| **English Lord, Ordinary Lady** *Fiona Harper* | 978 0 263 19743 3 |
| **The Playboy's Plain Jane** *Cara Colter* | 978 0 263 19744 0 |
| **Executive Mother-To-Be** *Nicola Marsh* | 978 0 263 19745 7 |
| **A Single Dad at Heathermere** *Abigail Gordon* | 978 0 263 19746 4 |
| **The Sheikh Surgeon's Proposal** *Olivia Gates* | 978 0 263 19747 1 |

## HISTORICAL

| | |
|---|---|
| **A Compromised Lady** *Elizabeth Rolls* | 978 0 263 19781 5 |
| **Runaway Miss** *Mary Nichols* | 978 0 263 19782 2 |
| **My Lady Innocent** *Annie Burrows* | 978 0 263 19783 9 |

## MEDICAL™

| | |
|---|---|
| **The Doctor's Bride By Sunrise** *Josie Metcalfe* | 978 0 263 19828 7 |
| **Found: A Father For Her Child** *Amy Andrews* | 978 0 263 19829 4 |
| **Her Very Special Baby** *Lucy Clark* | 978 0 263 19830 0 |
| **The Heart Surgeon's Secret Son** *Janice Lynn* | 978 0 263 19831 7 |

**MILLS & BOON**
*Pure reading pleasure*

1107 Gen Std LP

# DECEMBER 2007 LARGE PRINT TITLES

## ROMANCE

| | |
|---|---|
| **Taken: the Spaniard's Virgin** *Lucy Monroe* | 978 0 263 19503 3 |
| **The Petrakos Bride** *Lynne Graham* | 978 0 263 19504 0 |
| **The Brazilian Boss's Innocent Mistress** | 978 0 263 19505 7 |
| *Sarah Morgan* | |
| **For the Sheikh's Pleasure** *Annie West* | 978 0 263 19506 4 |
| **The Italian's Wife by Sunset** *Lucy Gordon* | 978 0 263 19507 1 |
| **Reunited: Marriage in a Million** *Liz Fielding* | 978 0 263 19508 8 |
| **His Miracle Bride** *Marion Lennox* | 978 0 263 19509 5 |
| **Break Up to Make Up** *Fiona Harper* | 978 0 263 19510 1 |

## HISTORICAL

| | |
|---|---|
| **No Place For a Lady** *Louise Allen* | 978 0 263 19412 8 |
| **Bride of the Solway** *Joanna Maitland* | 978 0 263 19413 5 |
| **Marianne and the Marquis** *Anne Herries* | 978 0 263 19414 2 |

## MEDICAL™

| | |
|---|---|
| **Single Father, Wife Needed** *Sarah Morgan* | 978 0 263 19375 6 |
| **The Italian Doctor's Perfect Family** | 978 0 263 19376 3 |
| *Alison Roberts* | |
| **A Baby of Their Own** *Gill Sanderson* | 978 0 263 19377 0 |
| **The Surgeon and the Single Mum** *Lucy Clark* | 978 0 263 19378 7 |
| **His Very Special Nurse** *Margaret McDonagh* | 978 0 263 19549 1 |
| **The Surgeon's Longed-For Bride** | 978 0 263 19550 7 |
| *Emily Forbes* | |